I Heard You Were Looking For Me

Ray Sharp

Avid Christian Books

Lakewood, California

I Heard You Were Looking for Me

Avid Readers Publishing Group

http://www.avidchristianbooks.com

ISBN-13: 978-1-61286-140-1

Edited by Randy Zana

Cover design by Steven Swift

Printed in the United States

For Cyndy, who changed my life

by becoming my wife.

Acknowledgements

I would like to thank Steven Swift for a cover that demonstrates how art can be informative as well as beautiful.

I need to thank Skip Press for the first edit and some extremely valuable advice. His expertise provides an author with clarity and encouragement. It is with good reason that Skip is a literary legend.

David Dirmann provided inspiration and encouragement at a time when I needed it most. His generous nature and artistic awareness are gifts that support an artist and I am grateful for his input.

I am also grateful to the staff at the Nixon Archives. The treasures I discovered there were simply not available anywhere else, and it was a great thrill to page through history using primary sources.

The Ford Motor Company, 7-Eleven, The Crab Cooker and The Rock Bottom Brewery all provided inspiration and support, which will become obvious as you travel through the narrative.

I would be remiss if I did not also thank the great movie and television star Betty Garrett for her gracious support. Despite my lack of reputation, she invited me into her home and shared inside information about the blacklist period and the characters involved. It is a tragedy that the blacklist interrupted her great career, but her brilliant work lives on in DVDs and other recordings of her performances.

Randy Zana has a bottomless reservoir of taste, talent and support that he shares generously. He is my cousin, and you might say we have collaborated since we were in the cradle. He has devoted a great deal of time and effort to the success of this book, and it was a joy to work with him. I look forward to many more collaborations.

Author's Note

This is a work of fiction, but many of the characters and events portrayed in this story are a matter of historical record. Anything the characters say or do within these pages can be attributed to the rambling imagination of the author.

Table of Contents

This Book was written in Black and White

PRELUDE
The Big Bang

I felt the explosion from my hiding place.

I remained hunkered down behind the Plymouth removing my handcuffs; missing most of the steaming purple glop that was raining from the skies. When I got up, I noticed a pair of loafers was stuck to the ground at the epicenter of a purple and orange blast mark extending about twenty feet in diameter. It looked as though a rocket had been launched out of those shoes.

The Crown Vic and the cab were branded with similar evidence of an explosive, destructive power, and the entire intersection was a symphony of purple droppings, flaming glop, and shrapnel from shattered Slurpee cups.

The cops both stood there like statues with blank expressions on their faces. They looked like they had been dipped in purple and singed with a blowtorch. I wanted to say, "I told you so," but when I saw their pathetic, terrified faces, I couldn't bring myself to do it.

The faces that had previously been so hard and cocky were now trembling in fear. The posture that had been so erect was now limp with apprehension, and the pants, which had been so crisply pressed, were now soiled with, well; let's call it the residue of fear.

Actually, that's a pretty good name for a book. I'll have to remember that. My name's McCoy; Joe McCoy, and I'm a bad novelist. You may have seen my books for sale in a used book store or a drugstore with a poorly-stocked paperback section. The covers all feature a naked blonde holding a knife, which never really had anything to do with the story, but it really looked cool. Most people in the know told me that buyers were only interested in the blonde, and they were probably right. She was shapely and scary and you couldn't tell if she was going to love you up or put you down. She was one hot blonde.

But, I digress. When I say I'm a bad novelist, I mean my books are bad, as in, they stink. At least that's what my last publisher told me. But I was making a pretty good living at it for a while.

A short while.

Back at the scene of the crime, I had slipped easily out of the handcuffs and stashed them in my pocket. Then I guided the coppers into the back seat of their cruiser and jumped into the driver's seat. I was pulling away from the scene of the crime when both the Crown Vic and the cab exploded in synchronized balls of flames big enough to rival the fireworks across the street at Disneyland.

I was in a police car, so it was impossible for me to resist the lights and siren. As a result, I was soon speeding down the street forcing motorists to pull over and watch me pass. The trip to the Harbor Station gave me a chance to see how the other half lived. When I returned the car and coppers I expected some gratitude. I thought they would welcome me with open arms, but the detective in charge had other ideas.

CHAPTER ONE
The Residue of Fear

I knew what they were thinking.

In spite of my altruistic efforts, the cops at the station still shoved me in a room with the two goo-covered coppers I had rescued from certain death; only instead of thanking me they were treating me as if I had caused the whole thing.

The coppers were supposedly guarding me, but the terror in their eyes indicated they were not guarding anything; not even the fact that they were terrified.

I knew exactly what terror looked like. Except in my case I had been given a little time to get used to the way things worked in the spiritual world before stuff started blowing up all around me. These two coppers were just trying to write a ticket when their whole world went kaboom. They were probably in shock. They were also probably wondering, "What is that horrible smell?"

They both stood silently across the table from me, trying without success to ignore the smell, and trying with even less success to look tough.

Tough was out of the question for these two.

Both coppers were covered from head to toe in the same gooey, sticky substance with which I had become somewhat familiar. This particular glop

1

was a thick, smelly, muck that looked like industrial jelly and smelled like the inside of a wet dog.

The most casual observer could see that their day had not gone well.

Both cops wore the official blue uniform of the Anaheim Police Department, but it was barely visible under all the glop. Steam continued to filter up off of their shoulders, exaggerating their shaky stance and skanky smell. These coppers seemed to have fallen back on their training and stood at parade-rest, but both of them rocked back and forth involuntarily. Their eyes stared off into the distance, at nothing in particular. I noticed one of them had an itchy finger that continued to pull an imaginary trigger, in spite of the fact that his gun was safely holstered.

They were trying desperately to appear strong and in control, but it was simply impossible to do so while looking and smelling like they did; and after what they had been through, it would be a long time before either of them was truly in control of anything again.

Meanwhile, I sat handcuffed to a cold metal chair. My shiny black suit was wrinkled and dirty, my white shirt was covered with dirt and blood, and my loafers were a mess, but my high and tight military crew cut was still standing at attention and I had managed to avoid any trace of the infamous glop. (After a while you learn where to stand.) I smiled at the coppers for a while to throw them off balance, but that just seemed cruel, so I spent the remainder of my time looking around the interrogation room. I had also gotten into the habit of planning escape routes.

The room was nothing like the ones you see in the movies. You always expect to see a dark room, filled with fedoras, and lit only from a blazing overhead lamp. That is a great image, but not an accurate one. In my experience, most interrogation rooms have mealy fluorescent lighting, dirty linoleum tiles, and a crummy metal table that rocks when you lean on it. Also, I have never seen a cop wearing a fedora in my life. In my opinion, the police could beat a lot more information out of perps if they would watch a few old movies before they design these things.

It wasn't long before I looked through the little window in the metal door and noticed Detective Dick Jones approaching. He peeked into the room and smiled a smirky kind of smile designed to make me believe he knew something I didn't. I wondered why he didn't just open the door and come in, until one of the uniforms saw him and opened the door for him. Then he sauntered into the poorly lit interrogation room as though he had just won a million dollars on Jeopardy.

The first thing you noticed about Jonesey was that he dressed well. I was used to detectives who always wore plaid sport coats with white tube socks peeking out over ugly black shoes. Jones obviously had a Nordstrom card. His suit was cashmere and his tie was silk. He even had a neatly folded handkerchief tucked into his breast pocket. It was no wonder that he kept his hands in his pockets and his eyes on me while he stood just inside the door.

Jones was doing pretty well with the resources that nature had given him. He was in fairly good shape, his short haircut made the most of male pattern baldness, and his eyes were light brown and piercing. Whether or not he had worked to develop his cop glare, it was effective. The stare made you want to look away.

His attention was first directed to the uniforms. He removed the handkerchief from his pocket and used it to reach into a briefcase that I hadn't previously noticed and pulled out two reports covered in purple fingerprints. Using the handkerchief as insulation from the reports, Jonesey tossed the reports onto the metal table with a certain flair and then adjusted the handkerchief with a whip of one hand and stuffed it back into his breast pocket. I didn't know how he did that, but it looked like something Clark Gable would have done at MGM in 1942.

He wasn't Gable, but he was just as crusty.

"You two rewrite this crap and take all the crazy out of it."

The officers looked at each other, then picked up the reports and started toward the door. Detective Jones then turned his glaring eyes toward me, but kept speaking to the coppers.

"And let's get ourselves a shower. This place smells bad enough."

The uniforms lowered their heads in shame and exited. Jonesey repeated his flourish with the handkerchief to pull the other metal chair from the desk. He insulated his hand from the chair arm with the hankie and deposited his backside into the seat. Then while whipping and tucking the handkerchief back into his breast pocket, he raised his legs onto the table, and crossed them at the ankles. The result was a relaxed image of the modern cop who was used to getting his way. I was afraid he was going to be harder to manipulate than the cops I was used to.

He managed to keep his eyes on me the whole time, and revealed a big smile that was the perfect metaphor for his confidence. I was used to cops who liked to think that everyone was looking at them while they preened around the room holding their stomachs in. Jonesey was too smart for that.

He intensified the glare. I was already staring at him, so we quickly had a real bad boy showdown. In my head, I could hear the soundtrack from a spaghetti western playing. At that moment, I was staring down every bully who had ever challenged me. I was primed for action and unwilling to take even the slightest bit of crap.

Then I noticed something about Detective Jones: he didn't blink, ever. I waited for him to blink, but he didn't, and as a consequence, I wanted to blink more than ever before, so I promised myself I wouldn't blink until he did.

Then I blinked.

Life is too short for games like that, and I couldn't help it. Who am I--Houdini?

But for some reason, my blinks cut the tension. He finally removed his hands from his pockets and slid a pack of Lucky Strikes across the metal table that divided us. I was still cuffed, so I couldn't reach for them, and that may have been part of his incentive, but I promised myself I wouldn't ask him to take off the cuffs. He removed one of the cigarettes and lit up. He inhaled deeply and I wanted a cigarette more than I wanted to get out of that room, but I told myself I would not ask for help no matter what.

Then I asked for a cigarette.

My desire for a smoke trumped my desire to win the little standoff we were having, so I motioned to the cuffs on my wrists.

"You mind?"

Pretending to be surprised, Jones smiled just like Joe Biden. He leaned forward, unlocked my cuffs and returned easily to his leisurely recline. Once comfortable, he placed a beautiful golden Zippo lighter on top of the pack.

I should probably tell you that I'm a nut for Zippo lighters. I've collected them for years, and when I say, collected, I mean, stolen. I reached for the smokes and lit one, igniting the magic moment in my lungs that makes me want to go on living. Then, I suddenly felt better. All my cares and woes had been reduced by at least eighteen percent.

Detective Jones raised his arms like Fidel Castro. "Of course we're all very pleased to have Ernest Hemingway drop in on us like this," he announced, although he and I were the only ones in the room. I offered no response.

"Silent treatment, huh? You better start talking, pal..."

I offered no indication that I was in a mood to cooperate, then Jones craned his neck and loosened his tie.

"... Or I make life difficult for the girl."

I inhaled deeply on my Lucky Strike. It tasted like a good year for nicotine, and the hydrogen cyanide was also excellent. I felt better, so I picked up the beautiful golden Zippo and started opening and closing it. I like to listen to the sounds those lighters make. The sound of a Zippo opening and closing creates a Pavlovian response in me, so I can amuse myself for hours just snapping the cover open and shut. But I knew Detective Jones had me. I didn't want him to get tough with her, and I knew I was at the end of the road with this caper. When the man says ten, the fight is over, so I inhaled deeply, slid the golden Zippo into my pocket, and leaned back in the chair.

"I'm going to tell you a story, but you are going to have a little trouble believing it. I'm not sure I believe it myself."

"I love a good story."

"Just don't bother to tell me you don't believe me, because I'm telling you right now, you're not going to believe me."

Detective Jones took his coat off and draped it over the chair next to him. He rolled up his cuffs and interlaced his fingers behind his head.

How's it start?

CHAPTER TWO
My Career

While Detective Jones reclined across the table from me, I started telling my story. It all started when I was in the Army. I was sleeping with my Company Commander's wife.

"Was this part of your regular duties?"

"Sort of; Colonel Dunbar trusted me with everything, including keeping an eye on his wife while he was out with a lady friend. To me, it seemed only fair that his wife would have little fun while he's on the town. Looking back on it, I should have felt guilty about what I was doing, because the Colonel and I had been downrange together, and a certain amount of loyalty to one's comrades comes along with an experience like that. Once we got back to the states our duty was soft but our desire remained hard, so he got a girlfriend and I slept with his wife--a lot."

However, one day I got so used to sleeping with Mrs. Colonel Dunbar, I was actually *sleeping* with Mrs. Colonel Dunbar. That was the day the Colonel got home early and stumbled in on us. I was sound asleep and somewhere in my dreaming I heard a noise like, *thunka, thunka, thunka*. It actually sounded like an old Volkswagen I drove when I was a kid. I didn't realize you had to put oil in those things from time to time, and just before the rusty old bug blew up it made a sound just like the thunka-thunka sound that was going on inside my head that day.

In my dream I could see that old VW smoking and sputtering and the thunka-thunka noise was horrific. Then I thought I saw fireworks and I woke up. That's when I noticed that Colonel Dunbar's fists were pounding on my face.

Another thing you should know about me is that I like to fight.

I have always enjoyed it, but for some reason I don't like *starting* fights. It takes me a while to warm up to the idea, but there's something about being challenged that sort of gets my blood hot. I guess I like to prolong the experience. So when a punk challenges me in a bar, I generally ignore him while he's shooting off his mouth about my mother, which is ironic because I never knew my mother. Then I let the punk shove me around without responding. By this time, I can see him getting his confidence up, impressing his buddies, and it makes me laugh because I know something he doesn't.

See, I was a hot shot pugilist on the Army boxing team, so I didn't just *enjoy* fighting, I was good at it.

A shrink would probably attribute all sorts of antisocial nastiness to my behavior, but what do I care? Don't ask me why, but I got a kick out of turning the tables on these punks. Whenever I got into a scrape, the punk would generally shove me a little, then hit me a couple of times without much resistance, and by the time I got into the mood for a little punching, he was already worn out.

Once I was hungry for hitting, the fight usually didn't last long. That's what happened at the Colonel's house. The old man had been a bruiser in his day; a real tough soldier, but when he caught me with his wife he was way past his prime, and wasn't in very good shape, so when I finally woke up, he was already pretty winded.

Most people don't realize that throwing punches is hard work, especially if you're experiencing a fit of hysteria over a Sergeant sleeping with your wife. I saw the Colonel punching away at me, and then I got up and finished him with a single jab. I was planning to follow the jab with a knockout punch, but the Colonel went down on the set-up, so there wasn't much point.

But the next part surprised me. His wife, who had told me she loved me about three hours earlier, also started to get mad at me when her husband hit the deck. The next thing I knew, I was trying to get dressed while the wife was slapping and scratching at me. It hurt my feelings a little, but it seemed like it would have been inappropriate to mention that. I was always pretty bad at ending relationships, so this was no big deal, but I knew I was in trouble with the Army.

Ironically, I loved the Army; in fact I still do. It surprised me more than anyone, but I had found a home as an American Soldier and I figured I would always wear the green. But the military police showed up at my room about twenty minutes later. Ten minutes after that I was in a five by ten cell that would be my home for the next six months. It wasn't actually so bad; in fact you could probably rent that cell for five grand a month in Manhattan. I put my feet up and stared at the bars in my window. About the time the thrill of that activity was wearing off, I got a package from the Mother Superior.

"The Mother who?"

"Okay, maybe I better back up a little more, unless you're in a hurry."

"Are you kidding? I'm riveted. Please, proceed."

I fired up another Lucky Strike and inhaled deeply. Detective Jones was stirring a cup of coffee that appeared to contain just the right amount of cream. I couldn't figure out where it had come from. I was thinking about asking for one myself when he made a circular motion with his fingers, beckoning me to continue.

I never knew my parents. I grew up in an orphanage just outside of Vegas. I used to tell people that I was the illegitimate son of Bill Clinton. My story was that Bill had indulged in a quickie with a University of Arkansas cheerleader, which, let's face it, isn't that hard to believe. In my scenario, I was conceived backstage at a *Carter for President* Rally in 1976, and the only time *Dad* came to see me was when he made secret gambling trips to Vegas. The kids at the orphanage ate it up with a spoon. Half the girls I knew said I had his eyes.

My real parents were probably a couple of kids who bottomed out in Vegas and didn't want to bring home a reminder of their losing streak. I figure I'm living proof that what happens in Vegas *stays* in Vegas.

Like most of the kids at the orphanage, I got in a lot of trouble, but the nuns always cut me a little extra slack for some reason. Don't ask me why. I really had the Mother Superior conned. I cheated in school, I gambled with the offering money and I got blotto on the sacramental wine, but she never really pounded me. I mean, she punished me, but not like the stories you hear about the penguins with those yardsticks.

I was riddled with guilt for years about the way I mistreated her. Well, riddled is probably overstating it. I knew I was a sinner, but it never kept me awake at night. I didn't believe in God or anything like that, so it was just a matter of working the system. Yeah, I really had the Mother Superior conned, or so I thought.

It turned out she conned me.

She liked the stories I wrote for class assignments, and I could usually get out of a punishment if I would write an essay or a short story. Since I was always in trouble, I was always writing and researching. One of my college professors told me that is why I had such a distinctive writer's voice. Of course the grammar and the spelling had to be perfect or no deal, but it came easy to me so what the hell?

She pushed me to write, and the next thing I knew I had qualified for a college scholarship with all of the stories I had been writing. Looking back on it, I guess she was playing rope-a-dope with me; hanging onto the crummy package until she knew I would be bored enough to finish it.

"Package? What package?"

"It was a pulpy novel I started in college."

"A novel? Did it get published?"

"Like college, it remained unfinished."

"What was it called?"

It was called, *The Taste of Blood*, which I thought was the perfect bad title for a bad first novel. I couldn't believe she had saved the crummy manuscript and tracked me down. I stood there holding it for a few minutes, then threw it into the corner. I didn't touch it for a few days. I really believed I could avoid getting back into bed with the Muse, but I finally got tired of staring at the walls and got to work. Day after day I found that working on the book was ten percent less horrible than counting the blocks in the cell walls. After six months, I was typing *The End* when they handed me an honorable discharge and showed me the door.

"An honorable discharge after what you did?"

"It seems my time downrange had an impact on my status."

"Downrange?"

"It's no big deal."

"Iraq or Afghanistan?"

"Afghanistan."

"What happened?"

"I'm telling you it was no big deal."

"It was big enough to overcome your crimes and misdemeanors."

"It was nothing."

What was wrong with me? I had no idea why I wouldn't tell Jones what I had done in Afghanistan. I had been decorated for valor and that medal kept me from receiving a dishonorable discharge several times, including the last incident with the Colonel. But after a lifetime of bragging about my exploits I had suddenly developed a serious case of modesty, or some other malady. Jones had to have a pretty good idea of what I was keeping from him, but for some reason I couldn't tell him about Afghanistan.

"You're really not going to tell me?"

"We will now return to our regularly scheduled programming. Like I said, they let me out. The Colonel was sitting at my desk when I got back to my room. I thought he might want another shot at me, but he smiled and shrugged when I came in.

"What can I tell you, Mac? I lost my head. I was wrong."

"Don't worry sir. I enjoyed the rest."

He may have been ticked when he caught me but he hadn't been wrong. Why couldn't I tell him that? I should have apologized to him for violating his home, but I couldn't do that either.

"Look, Mac, you and I have too much history to let it end badly. I can rescind the discharge. You can stay in the squad at the same rank and we'll go back to business as usual."

It was what I wanted to hear, but I heard myself turning it down.

"No thank you sir. I could use a change of scenery."

The Colonel stood up and chewed his lip a little. I guess he was really hoping I would stay, but he was too tough to argue.

"Well, okay then."

The Colonel offered me a meaty hand of friendship, which I took. He was a big enough soldier to admit his mistake. I wish I had been.

Don't ask me why. I didn't want to graduate. I loved the Army, and I guess I loved the Colonel, but it was easier to leave my home than to admit I was wrong.

"What an asshole."

"Tell me something I don't know."

The next day I stepped off a bus in Hollywood. I had maybe three bucks in my pocket and my only possession with any value was the jacket I was wearing. It was soft, supple leather and had a big patch on the back that read, *Army Boxing Championships*.

In spite of my poverty, I walked right into an expensive restaurant where the coffee cost ten bucks.

Don't ask me why I do these things.

I find myself climbing out on a limb.

Anyway, I was staring at the menu when I noticed that big movie star; Brad Chadwick was in the booth next to me. I had never seen anyone like that guy. It's like his teeth were all lit up. Then I

15

noticed Brad was smiling at me, and he leaned over to my booth.

"You gotta tell me where you got that jacket."

"I gotta?"

"You gotta."

"I hit a guy."

"And you took his jacket?"

"Yeah, I guess. I won a boxing tournament when I was in the Army."

"That is so cool. Join us?"

Well, I changed booths and my new buddy Brad introduced me to an icy vixen sitting in the booth with him. Her name was Vivian Sloane. She was probably fifty, but still looked pretty good, except that she seemed to be frozen, like she wasn't in the same climate as the rest of us. But her features were fabulous. Her nose, eyes, and chin all looked like they had been perfectly sculpted--out of ice. She acted like she was annoyed when I sat next to her, which was ironic, because she was all smiles later that evening when I woke up in bed next to her at the Beverly Wilshire Hotel.

It turned out that Vivian was a literary agent, and she was married to some gay guy. However, she enjoyed the *Horizontal Mambo*, so she liked to keep a guy like me on the side, and when she found out I had a bad novel in my kick bag, I became her new project.

"You mean you were the boy-toy?"

"If you want to put it that way."

"I do. Ernest Hemingway, *boy-toy*."

"Whatever, but she sold my novel in about five minutes. Turns out the gay husband ran a publishing company, so it was a sweet little set-up. Go figure."

"Sounds like you were pretty lucky for a boy-toy."

"I get it. It's a very wry observation."

This brings me to the woman thing. As long as I can remember, I've had what they used to call *a way with the ladies*. Everyone from my high school guidance counselor to Vivian seemed to like something about me, and I have usually been able to exploit what they liked into some sort of benefit. In this case, I had an apartment, a car, and a publishing contract for two books before she knew anything about me. (Well, she knew one thing about me.)

Life was good. I had the soft, easy days I had always wanted. I had virtually no responsibilities, virtually no debt and virtually all the comforts my little heart desired.

Unfortunately, I also had virtually no scruples, so I couldn't help myself. I climbed back out on that limb again.

A couple of months later, Vivian walked in while I was giving dictation to her secretary.

"That sounds innocent enough."

"Does it?"

"No."

Vivian stormed out, and I think I actually *heard* my literary career wheeze its last breath. Don't ask me why I do these things.

"Why *do* you do them?"

17

"I told you not to ask me that."

"So what came next?"

I still had one more book on my contract, so I decided to knock out the manuscript fast enough to beat the electric bill. But I had forgotten that it took me a long stretch in the brig with no distractions to finish the first book. Now I lived in an ocean-front high rise in Long Beach, where every apartment came equipped with hot and cold running blondes. I was too busy to write, at least to write very much.

I started every day with the best of intentions; sitting down at my Selectric...

"Your what?"

"Selectric. You know, the IBM Selectric II; that's my preferred writing tool."

"Not a computer?"

I hate computers. I learned to type on the old Selectric the Sisters used in the office. I loved that clunky old machine. I think it's the *clackety clack* sounds that the keys make while you're creating the magic. Those dudes hit the paper like they really mean it.

Computers are too anemic for the profound thoughts I've got floating around in my head. Or maybe they're too profound for the anemic thoughts I've got in my head. Either way, I don't like 'em.

I can also thank the Selectric for getting me into the Army. After I got kicked out of the University for having an affair with my Romance Poetry professor, I tried to rip off an old Selectric from the University library. The thing is--they would never even have missed it since everybody else used computers. Most college students don't even know what a typewriter is. This one was covered with about ten years worth of dust, but I got caught by a security guard who overslept his shift and bumped right into me on my way out. He was smart enough to know that I shouldn't have been carrying a big hunk of machinery with *University Property* written all over it.

I also owed some money to a mobbed-up bookie, but I wasn't worried about that as much as the stupid typewriter.

"Wait a minute. You were in the mob?"

"Not me; the bookie was. A guy named Max Dimitrios."

"Sure, I've heard of him. Uncle Max."

"Right, well, the judge told me I could serve two years in jail or two years in the Army. Now I didn't know what the female situation would be like in the Army, but I knew it was a helluva lot better than it would have been in stir. The next day I got a police escort to MEPS."

"MEPS?"

"It stands for *Military Entrance Processing Station*. It's the place where they inspect you before they ship you off to Basic Training."

"And then two years after that you were sleeping with the Colonel's wife."

"Right, and six months after that I finished the manuscript of my second book, *Kiss My Bloody Lips*."

"That sounds as bad as the first one."

"I thought so too, but it was doomed from the start."

"What happened?"

First, I walked to my parking space one day and saw a tow truck repossessing my Lexus. Then, while I was waiting to hear from the publisher, I was beginning to feel fluffy, so I decided to make a trip to the gym, except I owed them money too, so I had to squeeze past the manager in a crowd of *Spandex*. Then while I was waiting for the fancypants aerobics instructor to get his mix tapes ready, I lit up a Lucky Strike.

"You were smoking inside the gym?"

Oh, I love to smoke. I'm not saying I like it more than sex, but I can't imagine sex without it. After I fired up the heater, everyone around me started waving their arms and complaining, but fancy-pants didn't notice, so he started the workout. I had never smoked in class before. I was jumping and lifting with a coffin nail dangling from my lips, which is kinda cool. At least it was cool until fancy-pants saw me and started a hissy-fit.

"You can't smoke in here!" He said.

He ran over and grabbed the cigarette out of my mouth. I pulled out another one and lit it while I was still running in place. Then fancy-pants stopped the music and got in my face again.

"I will have to ask you to leave."

"Just get back to the front, Judy. My muscles are getting cold."

The guy started pushing, which I ignored. I was really not in the mood, but he kept pushing and finally took a swing at me.

That was a mistake.

I caught his fist like it was a slow curveball in midair, and I held onto it so he couldn't get it back. When he struggled, I twisted it a bit for emphasis. He was grimacing, and I was starting to feel less like an eccentric and more like a bully, so I let go of his hand and tossed the butt into the water fountain.

The guy started rubbing his wrist and looking at me like I had killed his puppy. He walked back up to the front, started the music and we all got a nice workout. Then I decided to take a steam.

I was just getting comfortable in the steam room when I heard a voice over my shoulder.

"Good afternoon, Mr. McCoy."

I looked up to see a well-groomed, handsome man sitting above me. His towel looked like it had been ironed onto his body, and he wore some very expensive-looking flip-flops. I didn't know him, and he seemed a little glamorous to be collecting dues for the club.

"My name is Carson Dillingham, Vivian's husband."

CHAPTER THREE
My Ex-Girlfriend's Gay Husband

Carson Dillingham was the type of guy who made most of us feel underdressed. Even sitting in a steam room wrapped in a towel he looked like he had been coordinated by experts. He had the kind of chiseled physique that you can only get with a personal trainer, and his haircut probably cost more than my best suit. Everyone else was sweating and sloppy, but somehow this guy seemed refreshed. I greeted him with all the politeness I could muster.

"I've been waiting to hear from you."

His smile revealed a lot of teeth and an absence of empathy.

"I read the first ten pages."

Then the dude just sat there looking smug. Anybody else would have just told me, but he was going to make me ask. It's all politics with some people.

"And?"

And I will never forget the arrogant look he had in his eyes when he spoke.

"Hated it."

I should have seen it coming from a mile away, but for some reason I was hoping this jerk wouldn't act like all those other jerks.

"Would you like to know why I hated it?"

"I don't think so."

"Then you will please return my ten-thousand dollar advance."

"Now wait a minute."

"It's a shame really, because your first book showed *such* promise."

I was sitting there like a moron while he got up and headed for the door. My life flashed before my eyes. Actually, my apartment flashed before my eyes and I didn't know where I would sleep if I didn't make a little scratch off the writing. I got between him and the door, which I think he took as a come-on until I started yelling.

"Wait a minute. I've got a contract."

"Yes, I checked it this morning. It specifically describes your advance as being dependent upon our *acceptance* of the intellectual property."

"Are you saying you don't accept?"

His eyes narrowed as he made with all the teeth.

"I don't know why everyone calls you stupid."

I didn't bother to argue. I know when I've heard the man count ten.

"I'll need a few weeks to get the money together."

"I'll give you until Monday."

"Today is Saturday."

"So it is. Ta."

He winked at me in a way I didn't like and walked out of the steam room toward the upstairs lockers. I stepped out of the steam and into a Lucky Strike.

After a shower, I was on my way out of the gym, thinking things couldn't possibly get worse when the manager and the sissy-boy aerobics teacher jumped in front of me. Fortunately, I was deeply immersed in my cigarette and therefore able to ignore them completely. One of them grabbed the back of my shirt, but I didn't feel like dancing.

"Not tonight guys; I've got a headache."

My expression seemed to convince them to back off. They both took a step back and stood silently. I continued out of the gym with no further molestation.

But my thoughts were disturbing. I needed a large infusion of cash, and I needed it fast. Then, when I got out on the street I heard some more *thunka-thunka* noises in my head. I realized that I had been jumped from behind.

Melvin Pistoia, who looked like an extra from *The Sopranos*, slammed me in the back of the head. I turned to see what hit me, and I got slugged from the other side by Leo Sinatra, who could have been Melvin's brother, except he's shaped less like a wrestler and more like a fireplug. I remembered these two from Nevada. They worked for Max Dimitrios, the bookie on whom I ran out, and this was the way they convinced people to pay their bills.

They were taking turns using me as their punching bag when I started warming to the idea of a little fisticuffs. Unfortunately, the initial blows had been good ones and I was woozy and bruised, but these two were such nasty characters that it didn't take long until I was hungry for hitting.

I head-butted Melvin and caught Leo in the crotch with my knee. Fighting against two guys is always a challenge. It's not like in the movies when one guy takes on a whole platoon, but I got lucky and dropped them both with my combination. I was hardly sweating and they were both on the ground moaning, especially Leo, who held onto his crotch as though he thought it would fall off. My work there seemed complete, so I leaned over to pick up my gym bag, but when I did, I heard the familiar click of a revolver. Melvin had pulled out a gun.

"Okay tough guy..."

"What? Don't you guys recognize the sanctity of winning a street brawl?"

"You owe Mr. Dimitrios money."

"Okay, you got me; I owe you five hundred bucks.

"Wrong, loser. That's what you owed when you went in the Marines."

"Army."

"Whatever. Since that time there's been interest, penalties, etcetera, etcetera..."

And as if on cue, Leo chimed in to finish the sentence.

"Etcetera!"

These two morons both displayed an extremely smug look, as though they were waiting for me to applaud. When I didn't, they took turns starting and finishing each other's sentences.

"So now you owe us..."

"...an even ten grand."

These guys were having fun. They were practically giggling, but I couldn't help them.

"You're gonna have to wait your turn."

"We'll give you 'till Monday..."

"...Or you're dead!"

"I hear that a lot."

Then Leo got a look in his eye like he had forgotten something.

"And then we're gonna kick your ass."

But something was wrong. They both stopped like there had been a disturbance in the force. Melvin was wide-eyed in astonishment. I was guessing that Leo had upstaged Melvin on his big line. He looked genuinely saddened, but mustered the strength for a big finish.

"Yeah!"

They took their attention off of me and stared at each other. I picked up my bag, and walked away, but I could hear them arguing as I did.

"I was supposed to say, 'kick your ass'."

"So what?"

"So, it's our signature style. You want a signature style, don't you?"

"Quit being such a baby."

"I'm not a baby. You're the baby."

"No you're the baby!"

"Oh yeah?"

"Yeah!"

Then Leo shoved Melvin and Melvin kicked Leo in the crotch. Soon, they were on the ground wrestling and arguing about who said what. I got out of earshot before they could start discussing choreography.

Later that night I was sitting on the balcony of my beautiful Long Beach high-rise apartment. I wanted to enjoy it before I got evicted, and I really loved watching the sunset. This particular evening, the sky contained beautiful patterns of clouds and leftover smog. It might burn your eyes during the day, but it was a gorgeous filter for the sun setting in the west.

After I finished my Lucky Strike, I noticed my Selectric sitting on the kitchen table. I turned my attention from the view to the typewriter, and started to take stock of my life.

Once again, I had fallen into lemonade and somehow reverted it back to lemon status. I felt like I had found a pot of gold and given it back to the leprechaun. I had, in essence, blown it, and I wasn't happy with myself. The old me would have shrugged it off and waited for the next thing to fall into my lap, but for some reason I couldn't do that this time.

The Selectric, my only conceivable ticket out, was waiting for me to make with the magic, if I had any left. I walked to the table, blew some dust off the last page, and hit the "on" switch. The old machine gurgled to life and sat sputtering like a lawn mower, so I sat down, popped my knuckles like a concert pianist, and lowered two fingers from each hand into the hunt and peck home keys. Then I made with the clackety-clack.

I was extremely surprised by what happened next.

I felt different somehow.

I wanted to spend some time writing, and I wasn't even in prison this time. I realized something about myself that I had been unwilling to consider before.

I enjoyed writing.

More than that, I was fulfilled by writing.

In fact, I realized that writing had been the only place in my life where I had felt any sense of satisfaction. Writing was the only positive thing I had ever done, and now it was about to be taken away, just as I realized how much it meant to me.

I stopped writing to think about my awakening, and when I did I wanted only to start writing again.

I pounded on the Selectric for hours. I went through the manuscript one chapter at a time. I threw out a bunch of crappy dialogue, fixed the structure, and crushed the keys to my heart's content.

That night was different. While I was fixing the problems with my book, I couldn't remember a time when I had had more fun. I felt pride, which was new for me. Who knew something this hard could make you so happy? My life was changed and it would never be the same, because after all these years I had finally found *my thing*.

By the time the sun came up, I had a new draft to show my ex-girlfriend's gay husband.

Then the phone rang, which surprised me; first because it was six AM, and second, because I sure hadn't paid the phone bill.

"Hello?"

I heard a sound on the other end of the line that could not really be called a voice. It was raw, husky and sounded more mechanical than biological, but I was able to discern the words.

"Mr. McCoy, this is Edyth Montgomery. I've just bought you and I want you to come to my office and meet with me."

"What do you mean *bought* me?"

"I mean I bought your contract from Carson Dillingham, so you now belong to me. The address is 8047 North Wilshire, Beverly Hills. Diablo Publishing, now get over here, chop-chop."

"I'll stop by tomorrow."

"If I don't see you in forty-eight minutes, my lawyers will see you in forty-nine. Now be a love and come see me."

I hung up the phone unable to process what was happening to me. On the one hand I apparently had a contract again, but the little man inside was telling me to run like the wind from this weird voice. I have never known an opportunity like this to actually work, and thinking about the voice on the phone, I shuddered to think what she would be like in person.

Then it occurred to me that Edyth might turn out to be just what I had been looking for. I looked at the stack of pages I had just completed in record time and thought that it might actually find its way to readers. Edyth would probably love the pages and maybe even give me a bonus. Yeah, that was the ticket. I celebrated my epiphany by spending five minutes leaning on a Lucky Strike.

CHAPTER FOUR
And Then It Got Weird

Edyth Montgomery's office was in one of those great big expensive buildings in Beverly Hills. But somehow it didn't seem expensive, it seemed dirty. The parking garage was especially rancid, and I remember thinking that all the spaces were at least ten percent too small for an average car. I had taken a cab, so I didn't have to worry about parking, but I noticed the grime while I was walking past the swarthy, Middle-Eastern guy sitting in the booth.

This was one of those joints where they charge you fifteen bucks to rent some concrete while you visit your lawyer. I felt creepy from the time I started listening to my footsteps echo off of the Chevys and Chryslers. These places are never really clean, but this one seemed to display every form of trash known to man; from used condoms (why anyone would use them in a garage remains a mystery) to stuff even more repulsive, it could all be found in the parking garage of Diablo Publishing.

Naturally, Diablo was on the top floor. In fact, this publishing empire occupied the *entire* top floor, but it was not the sort of place in which I wanted to spend any time. The lobby walls were all adorned with enlarged book covers, and I noticed a familiar theme emerge. Titles such as, *Lose 20*

Pounds in 20 Days, 30 Days to Financial Security and *Find Your Perfect Match in 14 Days*.

There was no one sitting at the reception desk, in fact I hadn't seen another human since the swarthy parking guy. I started to open the door leading into the offices, except somebody opened it for me. Somebody I couldn't see. But, when I got to the other side, there was nobody there. I figured Edyth had an automatic door opener; either that or the joint was haunted. I didn't much like either option, but she owned my contract, so I decided to enter the magic kingdom.

Then I heard that voice again.

Even though it wasn't new, her voice took a lot of getting used to. I still couldn't compare it to anything else in nature. The closest I could come was a rusty tin can being scraped along the backside of a cat. She was talking, a lot, but I couldn't tell you what she was saying because all I could hear was the Surgeon General's warning about cigarettes. I finally figured out she was trying to guide me back to her office.

"Joe? I'm back here darling."

Okay, I thought, but which way was back? Then she started guiding me like she could hear what I was thinking.

"It's this way precious. Turn to your left at the fern."

She seemed to have an amazing intuition, I was willing to give her that, but what was I getting myself into? I mean, I was used to taking chances, but this was a little too kinky. And what did she mean by fern? All the plants at Diablo Publishing were dead! That place didn't have another human in sight, or even another life form since all the potted plants had long since kicked the proverbial bucket.

"Keep going Lamb. Now you're on the right track."

I thought she must have been watching me on a security camera or something. I didn't see any cameras; I assumed she had them hidden, probably in the dead plants.

"That's my Joey. You're almost home."

I followed the awful sound into a wide-open office in the corner of the building, but I just wasn't ready for what I saw when I saw her.

She was sitting behind an enormous desk overlooking a beautiful panorama of the city. I kept my eyes on the panorama, because it kept me from looking at her. I've seen some tragic sights in my life, but I wasn't prepared for the sight of Edyth Montgomery. Her skin was like a catcher's mitt after it had been left out in the backyard too long. And she was wearing a hysterically bad wig, which I was guessing, was made from some sort of petroleum product. Her makeup would have made the students at the clown college say, "too obvious," and although she was at least fifty pounds overweight, she wore a tight-fitting, plunging neckline that revealed way too much. For the first time in my life, I wanted to see *less* of a woman's charms; a lot less. She swiveled back and forth in a continuous semi-orbit on a leather desk chair. I observed that the leather in the chair seemed more like human skin than her own.

I still couldn't bring myself to look at her, but out of the corner of my eyes, I could see Edyth open her arms to beckon me in a grand, operatic gesture, which belied her earlier threats of litigation. Once she began waving her arms I bounced my field of vision off of the pulsating flesh that drooped from her flabby arms. I was desperately searching the skyline for a landmark I could recognize, but she seemed intent on us becoming dear friends.

"Joe darling, come over here you little scamp and let me kiss you."

"I'm sorry, that wasn't part of my contract."

Silence filled the room and her face dropped to the floor. I returned my gaze to the picture window and embraced the quiet. Suddenly, she broke into a booming laugh, which was startling in its hacking, coughing, cat-scraping creepiness, and then she transitioned into a coughing fit that made me think the whole block should be quarantined. Between coughs she offered me a cigarette, and I declined; another first. She lit up the latest in a long line of Virginia Slims and pushed herself out of her chair. To my great consternation, my eyes were drawn to her disgusting, catcher's mitt cleavage as she contorted and slid across the leather chair. The chair made the usual flatulent squeaks and squawks, providing a soundtrack accompaniment perfectly appropriate to such a distressing moment.

I found myself cursing my eyes for looking. I quickly looked away, but feared I would never get the sight of her plunging, sagging bosom out of my head.

I felt weak. I walked to the window and leaned my forehead against it, watching the steam from my breath form on the window provided some solace, but this chick was really hard to take. If I had believed in God, I would have prayed.

But God was definitely not providing me with any relief. Edyth uncoiled a perfectly manicured hand, complete with blue veins and orange skin. She wrapped an arm over my shoulder and squeezed it. That was more than I could take, and I jerked away. Trying not to look at her, I had to make her understand my point of view.

"Back off Elvira, you bought my contract and that's all."

She stood staring at me for a moment in silence. At least I think she was staring at me. I couldn't tell because I was staring out the window. Then she started in with the scary laugh again, alternately laughing and coughing.

"Note to self," I thought, "quit smoking."

She managed to get through the laughter with a minimum of hacking, then ka-thumped flatulently back into her leather chair, still giggling.

"Sit down, my darling. Let me look at you. I can see why Vivian was so taken with your *writing*. You are adorable. Sit down."

I sat down, but I was ready to take my chances with her lawyers.

"I can see you want to get right down to business. That's too bad. I bought your contract because I saw something in you that I wanted."

"Great," I thought, this was my chance. I carefully placed the new draft on her desk. "Yeah, about that, I think if you'll have a look at the second draft of my manuscript, you will see that I fixed any problems I might have had with the first draft."

Without even looking at it, she used an orange, blue-veined hand to drop my manuscript unceremoniously into the wastebasket next to her desk. She inhaled her cigarette like she was sucking oxygen, reached completely over an enormous, butt-filled ashtray that took up a whole corner of her big desk, and dropped the Virginia Slim stub in on top of my manuscript. The book ignited like it was soaked in kerosene. Then she lit another cigarette and turned to me, not bothered in the least by the roaring trash can fire so close to the artificial strands in her wig.

"Look around you Joe. We don't do this type of book here at Diablo publishing." Then with a large, proud smile on her face, she somehow willed me to look into her eyes and said, "We publish crap."

"Crap?"

"That's right, crap. I have sold ten million books filled with crap; ten million books that have never been read."

"How do you know?"

"Don't be silly, dear boy. Look at the titles. These are *self-help* books. No one ever reads these things. *Improve Your Credit Rating In Seventeen Days?* My Goodness the public is gullible, and we take full advantage of that. Buying the book makes these losers feel better about themselves, but actually losing weight or cutting up credit cards requires a much bigger commitment. The good news for us is that even though our customers don't read this year's book, they don't hesitate to buy another one next year. Crap has been good to me, dear boy, and now, crap has been good to you as well."

"So you want me to write one of these crap books?"

"Oh, heaven's no, my darling. Your assignment is something much more prestigious. I want you to write a biography of distinguished former congressman, J. Parnell Thomas."

She might as well have said she wanted me to write about her uncle Gustav, the inventor of the automatic skin leatherizer. I looked at her like she was speaking Greek. I had never heard of former Congressman J. Parnell Whatsisname, in fact I couldn't have told you who my own congressman was.

Edyth seemed to sense my confusion.

"You do know about J. Parnell Thomas don't you dear boy?"

"I wouldn't know him if he sat in my lap."

She gave me a look that said, *tsk-tsk.*

"You went to public school, right?"

I rolled my eyes, but Edyth never slowed down.

37

"Nevertheless, I have a feeling about you dear boy, and I just know you are the right man for this job."

She blew a kiss at me and I swear I heard it cough as it zipped past my ear.

"Call me in two weeks when you have a first draft."

"Wait a minute. I don't know how to write a biography. I'm a novelist; a bad one."

"Well, you had better learn to write non-fiction quickly, because the word is out about you in the publishing game, and if you don't deliver this time, you will have to go back to the Marines."

"Army."

"Whatever."

She smiled like a cartoon cat and lit another Virginia Slim. She inhaled so deeply her cheeks looked like they touched inside her mouth. She seemed to gulp toxins at the end of her inhalation, then lowered her eyelids and turned away.

"Oh wait, you can't do that either, can you?"

Did she think I had been kicked out or did she know about my emotional struggle? Either way, she knew more about me than I wanted her to. She sucked another lungful of Virginia and held out an envelope full of cash.

"Here's two-thousand dollars for expenses. It will be taken out of your royalties, as will the advance that Carson paid you."

This was one of those moments. The ones you just know will haunt you the rest of your life.

I could take the money and hate myself or refuse it and live happily. I decided to tell her to shove her envelope full of cash and then sue me to her tiny little heart's content.

"Really?"

"Nah, I took the damn money. I just don't like to admit it."

I reached for the cash, still trying not to look at her, but I couldn't find it. I was feeling through the air, reaching in her direction while trying not to look at the scary old hag, but it was no use. No matter how I waved my hand around in her direction, I couldn't feel anything that felt like an envelope. Then finally, I felt the stupid cash and grabbed it, except she wouldn't let go. I had no choice; I turned my eyes in her direction and I was suddenly face to face with her. She had come around to my side of the desk and was now pressing up against me like a horny dog against a leg. She released the envelope as she moved toward me, and the next thing I knew, her face was stuck to mine and her tongue was boring into my mouth, traveling past my bicuspids. I tried to resist, but the old bat's tongue was more powerful than a python. I jumped back in shock and spit as hard (and as often) as I could, but it felt like her tongue had been halfway to my stomach before I did. My eyes became so wide that I got a comprehensive view of her shriveled, horrific features smiling at me.

She burst into her patented hacking laughter while I stomped out the door, past the dead plants and into the waiting elevator in the lobby.

"Great to be in business with you, dear boy," I heard her shout as the elevator door was closing. "Remember, the congressman was a great man, so treat him well."

I spent all night and the next morning gargling.

In the afternoon, I went to the library to check out this J. Parnell Whatsisname.

I walked in to the Main Long Beach Library and saw dozens of nerds camping out in front of computers, absorbing the optimal amount of radiation to achieve their computer geek pallor.

I hate computers.

All of a sudden, we're slaves to those stupid machines. You have to buy a new one every six months and you can't wipe your nose without the most recent version of the software. When the Selectric got hinky I could usually fix it by punching it a few times, but computers required you to actually read the manual. Take a look at the nerds staring at those gizmos some time. If it weren't for acne, they would have no pigment whatsoever.

But mainly, I feel like I'm cheating when I use a computer. I think a book written on a computer is a little synthetic; an artificial cloning of the writer's intentions. You can't notice the difference with your eyes; but you notice it with your heart. The words I write come from my soul, and to dig them out I need a tool that I can feel, that I can hear, that collaborates with me on a more organic level.

Plus, I just don't trust that Bill Gates guy.

Then, there's always the chick factor. I like to go to a library, absorb the words on paper, and then get a cute librarian to do the research for me. A blonde babe librarian with reading glasses really makes me melt, especially when she's stretching to retrieve a book from the top shelf. I scratch whatever information I need on a cocktail napkin, go home, make with the clackety-clack, then hook up with Marian the Librarian later that evening for a couple of tall cold ones. Life is good.

But this stupid book wasn't going to be so easy. This wasn't a mystery where I could make everything up. This time I had to get facts, and they had to be right. You can understand my dilemma.

I spotted the babe I was looking for working behind the reference desk. She was pretty, blonde, in her early twenties, and she typed at the speed of light. She smiled like a model when I approached the information desk. I noticed her nametag said, *Clarisse*.

"I'm looking for information about a former Congressman from New Jersey named J. Parnell Thomas."

She frowned as though I had told her that her poodle died.

"Have you tried Google or Yahoo?"

"I don't swing that way baby."

She smiled and wrote his name down on a scratch pad.

"What was his name? Thompson?"

"Thomas, J. Parnell."

"I've never heard of him."

"Tell me about it."

She went to her computer and started typing at the speed of light. She looked up after a moment.

"Well, there's never been a book written about him. How long was he in congress?"

"Thirteen years."

More speed typing.

"Wow, this is a tough one. I see a lot of hits, but not much real information. Oh wait; there is a scrapbook about him at the Nixon Library."

"Will they let me check it out?"

"No, it's in the archives. You can read it there and make notes."

"And where is the Nixon library?"

"Yorba Linda."

"Yorba Linda? What am I, a farmer?"

I obviously said something wrong, because Clarisse seemed to take offense.

"Hey, I live in Yorba Linda."

"Really, are you free for dinner?"

CHAPTER FIVE
The Nix

The next morning, Clarisse made breakfast and drove me to the Richard Nixon Library and Birthplace. The balmy landscape of Orange County was extremely calm, and while we cruised along Imperial Highway, I stared at the palm trees floating by and thought about J. Parncll Thomas.

You can understand how such thoughts would disturb me.

Here I was, cruising through palm trees and sunny skies with a beautiful librarian as my driver and all I could think about was some stupid congressman who died before I was even born.

The previous day, before I got Clarisse to knock off early, we discovered Thomas was not just a former congressman, but a disgraced former congressman. Apparently, he was a big shot in the forties who was chairman of something called The House Un-American Activities Committee, or HUAC for short. I guess the Communist Party had been trying to take over the country after World War Two, so the heavy hitters established a committee in the House of Representatives to keep the commies at bay. Anyone who was suspected of being a Communist was called to testify before that committee. Eventually, a bunch of the people found their names on a certain list, and that list prevented them from getting a job. They were blacklisted from working; at least from any good jobs. As chairman, J. Parnell had found a home.

At the time, it seemed like half the writers and actors in Hollywood were commies. He saw that as a big opportunity. Pretty soon, J. Parnell dragged a bunch of the Hollywood commies to Washington and made them hysterical during a special session of Congress. You can watch black and white film of these dudes going off at the Nixon Library. It's really quite amusing.

Before J. Parnell was done, he put most of the Hollywood commies out of work, and even put ten of them in jail for something called Contempt of Congress. Those ten dudes were known as The Hollywood Ten, but I had never heard of any of them. In fact, I always thought some guy named McCarthy was the big shot commie hunter, but apparently J. Parnell was bagging Marxists long before McCarthy. He was one of the most powerful dudes in Washington and Hollywood.

The ironic end to the J. Parnell Thomas story is that he wound up going to prison before the Hollywood Ten. It seems he was convicted of padding his own congressional payroll and they threw him into the same prison as a couple of the commies he sent up the river.

What a loser, I thought. Not only does this guy get caught with his hand in the cookie jar, but now George Clooney makes movies about McCarthy and no one's even heard of the dishonorable Mr. J. Parnell.

Clarisse told me that there are over 500,000 Google hits (whatever those are) for this guy, but they all have the same two paragraphs. It's like all important records of this dude got erased from the world's hard drive. When you research him, you only learn enough to know that you don't know squat about J. Parnell Thomas. There are no books about him, there are no movies about him, and you can't even find embarrassing interviews where Edward R. Murrow makes him turn red. What a loser.

We pulled into the Nixon Library before the tourists started cluttering up the place. It's a warmer joint than I had expected. A clean, austere design, with lots of trees, fountains and flags; perfect for an overachiever like Nixon.

I smiled at Clarisse and leaned in for a goodbye kiss. I hate to generalize, but it has been my experience that Orange County girls are great kissers. Clarisse was a warm, intelligent woman with a homespun quality and a small trust fund. As she handed me her phone number, I knew I would never see her again.

As I inched away from her car, she opened those big eyes and batted them at me a few times. I know what you're thinking, but I already admitted that I exploit women; it's what I do. And I was completely honest with her.

"I had a really good time last night Bobby," she said.

Okay, maybe I wasn't completely honest, but in my defense, she guessed my name was Bobby. I just never corrected her.

"So, you'll be over to meet my parents on Saturday?"

"You bet."

Okay, I guess I deserve the tsk-tsking I can sense in your reaction. We kissed again and I got out, but before I could get away, she made one last leaner out the window.

"I think I love you."

And there it was.

She hit me with the love bomb.

Even I didn't like me at that moment.

But when you're a guy like me, you learn to get over things like that.

I plastered phony smile number seventeen onto my face as she drove away. I watched as she maneuvered her new hybrid past the big fountain and out of my life. Then I walked up the steps to the entrance.

Staring at the library, I saw Nixon's name carved into an impressive wall of granite. It was beautiful, but on second thought seemed to be too much somehow. Dick Nixon was a little punk who rose to become the leader of the free world by working menial jobs and pretending to ignore it when the rich kids insulted him. He managed to alienate a lot of people in spite of stuff he did like ending the Viet Nam war, opening up trade with China and holding the first ever rock concert in the White House. Well, it was actually The Turtles, but they're closer to rock than any other president had gotten.

When I looked at the Nixon Library, I imagined neighborhood kids picking on little Dick because he had to quit playing in the street to practice the piano, or work in his father's store, or do hours of homework. If I had been one of his neighbors I had no doubt in my mind that I would have made him cry. Well, at least I would have made him uncomfortable. This wasn't a guy whose name got carved in stone; this was a guy who had gravy stains on his tie. Standing there by the big fountain I felt shame for the times I had bullied kids like Dick Nixon, and then I felt compelled to rename his library. This place needed a name that was more like the man. Somehow that name came to me immediately.

The Nix.

The big name carved into the building is much too long and formal for a kid with dirt under his fingernails. The Nix would be welcoming, amiable, and much more user-friendly than the name on the wall. Of course it's doubtful that the museum staff would rename the place, but I can dream, can't I?

The atmosphere at the Nix is what I imagine the White House must be like, but with less security. It's big and solid enough to be impressive, but somehow humble too, as you might expect from a poor Quaker boy who had to earn a scholarship every time he got admitted to a new school.

Once they know you've got an appointment in the archives, they send one of the archivists to get you. After the first visit, I was convinced that archivist is Latin for man-hater. The gal who came to get me was an exercise in drab, and judging by her demeanor, archivists were discouraged from any sort of pleasantry. Her nametag said, Nancy, but her expression said, back off! The volunteers up in the gift shop had been exceedingly friendly, but those days were gone forever, and I was being escorted into the archive by a Nazi in sensible shoes.

Nancy the Nazi read me a few rules of conduct, and let me know she would brook no horseplay. Then she walked out and left me with thousands of books, all alone except for two other archivists who were also scrutinizing me. After a while, Nancy returned with a squeaky cart on which she was wheeling the scrapbook in 20 volumes. Calling it a scrapbook wasn't really accurate. The so-called scrapbook was a series of de facto piles, bundled, ever-so-carefully, into de facto volumes using de jure construction paper. The process requires a researcher like me to take a volume off the cart, open it up and start wading through the piles of information, which is substantial.

After five minutes with the first pile, I knew more about J. Parnell than I could have learned in all those Google searches, whatever they are.

He was born J. Parnell Feeney in Allendale, New Jersey, he was a Colonel in WWI, he sailed through college and the Wharton School of Business before a successful insurance career, and along the way he developed a real dislike of the New Deal and Franklin Delano Roosevelt.

J. Parnell started his political career with the odd letter to the editor, complaining about local and state officials with whom he disagreed. He even showed a wry, sarcastic wit when dealing with puffed-up politicos such as the New Jersey Governor who couldn't balance the budget. J. Parnell held a public Mathematics Class for the governor, who didn't show up. J. Parnell used the event to explain the realities of budgetary responsibility to the press, who did show up.

Soon, J. Parnell was the mayor of Allendale, and quickly thereafter an assemblyman. Then in 1937, a congressional seat opened up and our boy was chosen to fill it. Every year, he became more secure and influential in his position. He was appointed to the House Un-American Activities Committee in 1942, and became its chairman in 1946. That was the pivotal moment in Thomas's life, and catapulted him into the national spotlight, which he relished for a couple of years. He had no way of knowing that he would be banished from the spotlight so completely that he would be virtually erased from the nation's memory.

It was J. Parnell who came up with the idea of investigating Hollywood, and his personality fueled a national scandal, but it couldn't sustain his memory after order was restored.

Apparently gossip columnist Drew Pearson blew the whistle on Thomas for padding his payroll. Pearson reported that J. Parnell had a secretary on his staff who earned $2500 per year, except that the secretary didn't really work for him (at least not in the office), and she didn't really collect a paycheck, but the government really did pay out $2500, which somehow found its way into J. Parnell's bank account. They called it malfeasance in office, and it brought his career to a screeching halt.

That's why we don't refer to this period in time as *Thomas-ism,* or *The Thomas Period.* The biggest indicator that Thomas is forgotten is that virtually everything he did is now attributed to McCarthy.

Would a United States Congressman actually risk all his power and influence for $2500? It seemed like an absurd risk. I was pondering that concept when I was hit with a lightning bolt. Something made me look up from the scrapbook, and when I did, I saw a beautiful woman standing over me, and she was so radiant she forced all thoughts of J. Parnell Thomas right out of my head.

CHAPTER SIX
Phoebe

"What are you doing?" She demanded to know.

She must have been about 25, and there was something devastating about her that I couldn't categorize. She had a light olive complexion, dark black hair, and pouty, extraordinary lips. I had seen all of those before, but never in a combination like her. Something about her whole was greater than the sum of her parts. She was part Salma Hayek and part Audrey Hepburn, and I used that definition to explain the gurgly feeling inside my chest. I had seen beautiful before. Heck, I took beautiful for granted. This was different.

She had a figure like Jessica Rabbit, and I must have been reacting like one of those Tex Avery wolves that pounds himself on the head with a big hammer, because I had completely lost the ability to act cool. This added to my consternation, because I was supposed to be the take charge guy for cryin' out loud; but with her, I was chargeless.

Her dark eyes were large, unusually round, penetrating, and filled with fire. I got the idea she could see inside me, and I didn't like her looking in there. I felt naked. No, worse than naked.

I felt like she knew me.

I didn't know what to do because until that moment, I never realized that I didn't want anyone to know me. I wasn't sure I even knew myself, and I was damn sure I didn't want anyone else achieving that realization before I did. In any event, I believed that she saw right through all of the tricks in my bag.

I didn't know what to do. I could have almost believed there was something supernatural, or spiritual about her. She had something that rendered me speechless, and after all the experience I've had with women, that's hard to do. This is usually the moment in all of my relationships when I know whether or not I *want* a particular woman.

This one I wanted, and quickly.

Then I noticed something else about her: She was ticked off.

"What are you trying to pull?" She asked me between clinched teeth. (I forgot to mention she also had great teeth.) She was *whispering* in that special library *shout* people use just before they get kicked out.

"Huh?"

"You heard me."

"What are you talking about?" I asked. (At least, that's was what I was trying to ask. The condition I was in, I may have said "Unf-naga-doo-doo.")

"You know what I'm talking about," she growled.

"I really don't."

At that moment, I was holding a stack of carefully organized elements from the J. Parnell scrapbook. I had been returning them to the cart, and I was being a lot more careful than I normally am because I didn't want to incur the wrath of Nancy the Nazi. Still staring into this chick's voluptuous lips, she surprised me; she looked down at the stack of scrapbook pages and knocked them out of my hands, splattering them all over the floor with that *slappy* sound paper makes when it's struck with extreme prejudice.

When Nancy the Nazi saw what had happened, she slammed her pencil down onto the desk and stomped her sensible shoes over to where I stood, knee-deep in a pile of J. Parnell Thomas. She glared at me with blood in her eyes. Of course I didn't think Nancy was mad at *me*. I was slightly concerned that Jessica Rabbit would get kicked out for roughhousing, but then I turned to see all those beautiful features had disappeared, completely, without a trace.

Along with the beautiful body.

The Nazi was holding me completely responsible for the carnage at my feet.

I didn't know whether to curse the girl or admire her, but she was gone.

Nancy the Nazi started to pick up the papers and place them back in the correct order. I bent over to help her and she actually slapped my hand. I stood up and looked around. All of the other archivists were looking at me as though I had spilled maple syrup all over everything. I wrapped for the day and went looking for the mystery woman who had turned my world upside down.

"This was how you met the girl?"

"Are you gonna let me tell it or are you gonna keep interrupting?"

"Sorry. Please continue."

After a short search, I realized the Nix was closing, so I gave the parking lot a brief look, and then grabbed a waiting cab with instructions to return me to the comfy confines of Long Beach.

I told the driver to take me directly to the *Rock Bottom Brewery*. It's a nice joint that serves good food and strong beer. The long cab ride made it possible for me to relax and ponder what had happened. Once I arrived, I was comforted somewhat by a Tuscan chicken salad and a Pelican Red Ale. Before long, I sort of got lost in a high school basketball game playing on the local channel. It was slightly reassuring to sip the strong ale, but very disconcerting to think about the mystery woman at the Nix. Who was she? Why did she care about my research? Why couldn't I stop envisioning her naked? (I actually knew the answer to that one, but you can see how the question would frustrate me.)

Several Red Pelicans later, my eyes drifted down from the TV monitor to the bar, and I saw something that made me gasp.

She was sitting there.

The mystery woman who had caused me such grief was sitting at the bar, staring at me. This had to be a dream, I thought to myself, because there's no way this chick could be here in Long Beach. I have to tell you that I have never before wondered what to do in these situations. As a rule, I just charge right in, following my instincts, and it usually turns out okay.

For some unknown reason, I couldn't do that this time.

I started to get up, then I hesitated, and I never hesitate. I got mad at myself and jumped up from my seat, dropping my napkin on the floor. I bent over to pick up the napkin, and when I looked up again she was gone--again.

Who was this chick? Why was she haunting me? How did she move so fast? I turned to call for the check, and suddenly, there she was, just inches from my face, with a beautiful smirk I couldn't help but admire.

"Who are you?" I practically screamed.

"Aren't you going to ask me to sit down?" She purred.

This time, her voice was like hot caramel sauce being poured over ice cream.

"Please!" I blurted, but when I heard the squeaky pathos in my voice I tried again.

"Please!" The second time it sounded even more pathetic because it was obvious I was trying to take a Mulligan.

I was extremely conscious of the fact that after a lifetime of training myself to be the cool one, I was completely flustered, and hot lips across from me was the cool cucumber. It was sort of depressing, but I put my depression aside in hopes of finding out something about her. I glanced to where she had been sitting and noticed an empty tumbler. I breathed deeply; hoping to calm my nerves and summon up a bit of the old charisma.

"I'm guessing you're drinking a Grey Goose Martini on the rocks, with four olives, dirty."

She smiled and nodded. I couldn't tell if she was impressed or condescending as she squeezed into the booth.

"You're good, but the vodka is Absolut."

I signaled the waiter and ordered another round. I considered switching to coffee, but by this time I was irritated with my own self-doubt and continued with the Red Pelicans.

She seemed to be smirking at me, like she knew something I didn't, which she probably did, which made me even angrier. At the same time, I wanted to get into her pants so badly I could have dialed her phone number without using my finger.

"What was that all about at the Nix today?"

"The what?"

"The Nix."

"Oh, I get it. That's good," she said with more than a little condescension. I suppose your male ego requires you to reduce your subjects in order to inflate your own importance.

"Thanks," I replied with as much sarcasm as I could muster. "Why did you freak out at the Nix?"

The waiter came with our drinks. She lifted a toothpicked olive out of her glass and opened her mouth just wide enough to accommodate the round, green fruit, and then she wrapped her lips around it in a way that made me very jealous. Still, she said nothing.

"What do you care what I'm doing at *the Nix*?" (This time I emphasized my nickname hoping to rub it in, but I just felt foolish.) She just sat there looking fabulous, enjoying the moment, and knowing she had me.

"Get hold of yourself," I thought. "She has you playing by her rules. You have to bring the game to her."

When I'm right I'm right, and this time, I knew I was right.

So I threw caution to the wind, tossed three twenties on the table and got up to leave.

Amazingly, it worked.

"Don't go," she said. Her desperation showed for just a moment before she tucked it back into her alter ego, but I could see I had cracked her veneer. She was nervous.

"Why do you care what I'm researching?"

She hesitated for a moment like she didn't know what to say. I said nothing because my question was still hanging in the air waiting to be answered. Then she looked down like a child caught stealing candy and defiantly said, "That's my book."

"What's your book?"

"J. Parnell Thomas."

"*You're* writing a book about J. Parnell Thomas?"

She raised her head and again became defiant.

"Yes, and he's mine. You can't have him. Women have suffered as second-class citizens for far too long and I am not going to allow you to hijack my topic."

I smiled and sat down.

"Sweetheart, I don't want your topic, and I have no idea what the women's movement has to do with this. It's just a paycheck for me."

"You mean someone is *paying* you to write your book?"

"Well, yeah."

"But no one has ever written a book about him."

"Tell me about it."

"Damn!"

She just sat there, sucking on that stupid olive. "Why doesn't she just chew the bloody thing?" I wondered. I decided to find out what she knew. "So, how long have you been working on your book?"

"Thirteen months. It's a master's thesis, *J. Parnell Thomas: The Man History Forgot.*"

"Really, what school?"

"Chapman University."

"And what's your major?"

"Creative Writing."

"And how did you first get interested in J. Parnell Thomas?"

"About..." She looked up and shook her head. Whatever thoughts had taken her from me had disappeared and now she was back among the conscious. "You first," she said. "How did you first get interested in him?"

"I'm still not interested in him."

"How can you write a book about a man in whom you have no interest?"

"I'm interested in paying the rent."

"How long have you been working on it?"

"I started yesterday."

Suddenly, her eyes blazed with anger, and this chick's eyes were unusually hot! She also did this thing with her face that I would see again. She only turned her face about a quarter of an inch, but without changing expression she made me want to run and hide. It was a metamorphosis that only I could see. I was torn between my confusion and my ardor.

"Yesterday?" she said defiantly, "Yesterday? How did you find out about the scrapbook?"

"A librarian told me."

"Damn! Stupid librarians can't keep their mouths shut."

"What do you care if I write this book? I didn't even know who this guy was until yesterday morning."

"Why would they hire you?"

I said nothing. She looked at me like she could find the answer in my face. She looked me up and down, saying nothing, and seemed to come to a conclusion.

"You slept with the publisher didn't you?"

I had to think about it for a minute, and my hesitation seemed to disgust her.

"Jerk."

"Loser."

"Gigolo."

"Oh, that hurts," I said sarcastically, but to my surprise, it did hurt.

I tossed another two twenties on the table. Although I immediately realized I had now paid a hundred bucks for three drinks, I wasn't about to give her the satisfaction of watching me pick up the bills, even if I had to walk home. Then I leaped to my feet, calibrated the correct listing position for five Red Pelicans and drifted toward Ocean Boulevard.

Once in front, I poured myself into a cab and laid my head back against the seat, happy to have that whole experience behind me. After giving the driver my address, I drifted off to sleep, and I swear I was dreaming about this chick. I could see her in my dream taunting me with her beauty. That really got me angry.

But not as angry as when I woke up and found her sitting next to me in the cab. How did she do that? Was she a witch?

"How do I get rid of you?" I asked.

"I recognize you're angry."

"I'm not angry, I'm furious."

"I know I could have handled that better."

"Pull over driver," I said.

The driver started to pull over.

"He's kidding," she said.

The driver pulled back into traffic.

"I'm not kidding," I said.

The driver shook his head and started to pull over again.

"My husband likes to joke, driver," she said.

The driver pulled back into traffic, mumbling, what I'm sure were Arabic obscenities about stupid Americans. I considered jumping out the window.

"Look, maybe we could work together," she said.

I was intrigued with the idea of receiving the benefit of her research, and even more intrigued by the idea of receiving the benefit of her charms.

"Maybe. What did you have in mind?"

"We share information, don't duplicate efforts, and we each write our own book."

"Maybe." I wanted to think about it.

"Okay, then you can pull over driver."

"What is with you?"

"Isn't this where you live?"

I looked out the window to see the driver pulling up in front of my building. How did she know? I had given up speculating for that evening. I got out of the cab, and to my surprise, she followed me. Then I waited for her to leave, and when she didn't, I leaned my head toward the building in the universal gesture for, "Wanna come upstairs?"

We stepped into the elevator and I punched *10*. She looked at me and I looked at her. She reached up and gently touched the pearls around her neck as though she was trying to decide what to do. I had by this time completely given up wondering what to do, but I couldn't stop my eyes from staring into hers.

Suddenly, she lunged forward and I did the same. She grabbed me and wrapped her luscious lips around mine in an embrace that was more passionate than any in my previous experience.

Instantly, I felt urges and emotions I had never before realized. I wanted more of her, and fast. The elevator stopped at the fifth floor and another couple stepped in. At least I think it was a couple, because I never looked up from the festival of delight in which I was engaged. She was able to do things with her body, even while wrapped in a conservative suit that I had never known another woman to do, in any stage of dress.

I felt somehow like it was my first time, and more than that, I wished that it was.

The other riders got off at the eighth floor. I had gotten off around the second, but I wasn't finished. The kissing, groping, and feeling continued. It continued out the elevator doors at ten, it continued while unlocking my apartment door, and it continued into my kitchen. We banged into the elevator door, we banged into the wall in the hallway, and we banged into the threshold of my door. In the kitchen, I hoisted her onto the marble counter top and into my permanent lovemaking hall of fame. I anticipated a night of passion such as had never been experienced by homo sapien, until a funny thing happened, she stopped.

Just like that.

"We better stop," she said.

"Huh?"

"We've got to stop."

"Why?"

"You know why."

"I don't know why." "I know why I stopped when I was twelve, no ten, no..."

"This is as far as I go."

I hadn't had a girl pull this one on me since I was twelve, no, ten, no--well, I hadn't ever experienced it before, but I had heard of it, and I didn't like it.

"Are you serious?"

"Yes, it's very nice, but it has to stop before we get carried away."

"Carried away? Carried away? I'm already carried away. I was carried away in the restaurant. I am hours past carried away."

"Well, I don't believe in sex outside of wedlock."

"Wedlock? Wedlock? What ever happened to all that women's rights crap you were giving off before?

"I recognize the apparent contradiction."

"This is more than a contradiction, it's a crime."

"Sorry, but I'm a Christian."

"So what? I've slept with hundreds of Christian girls."

As the words were leaving my mouth, I realized I had my foot in it. She just stared at me in a way that made me feel small, in more ways than one. Those eyes that had been so alluring were now vacant and filled with a message that said, "Closed for business."

"It must be rough to get shot down for the first time."

"Tell me about it."

I was in uncharted waters, but I was reevaluating this chick as we stood there in my kitchen.

"Look... hey, what is your name?"

"You mean you were prepared to sleep with me without even knowing my name?"

I had also done that many times, but when she put it like she did, it sounded dirty somehow.

"Name please?"

She stood there looking at me saying nothing. After a lifetime of not caring what women do, I suddenly had to know what was going on in her mind.

"Her name was Phoebe Valdez."

"Well I know that now too. Where were you when I needed you?"

"Tell me about her."

She was like the religious *left*. I had never seen it before, but nothing about this chick seemed to fall into the *normal* category. I walked onto my balcony overlooking the Pacific Ocean, the Queen Mary, and the tankers in Long Beach Harbor. I sat down and fired up a much-needed Lucky Strike. She stood next to my chaise lounge.

"You know, for a Philistine, you're a pretty good kisser."

I ignored her words and placed my hand on her waist. She removed it and walked to the refrigerator. After looking inside, she turned my way and shook her head.

"I take it you eat out?"

She brought two beers to the balcony, opening hers and setting the other on the table just out of my reach. I left it there, not willing to let her see me squirm.

That lasted about two seconds.

I wanted a beer and I was out of my league when it came to playing head games with this chick. I stood up, walked to where the beer sat, opened it and returned to my chaise.

"So tell me about the honorable J. Parnell."

"Honorable, that's a laugh. He was a right-wing witch hunter. He sent the Hollywood Ten to prison, and he got caught embezzling funds from his own congressional budget."

"Okay, the Hollywood Ten were the commie screenwriters who were putting propaganda into the movie scripts?"

"It's not against the law to be a communist."

"But they didn't go to jail for being commies. They went to jail for contempt of Congress."

I must have stung her a little with that one, because her expression changed from cocky to worried. This chick was smart, and beautiful, and somehow supernatural, but she couldn't play poker."

"You are an idiot."

"Relax, Doll Face, I'm probably gonna be on your side, but if I have to write this miserable book, I need to write the real story, not the spin. Why do you want to write this book, anyway?"

"Because it's my master's thesis and all the normal subjects were already taken. My thesis advisor said he wouldn't read another McCarthy book. He said McCarthy's been done to death."

I wanted to see what she knew about McCarthy so I played dumb.

"You know, Joseph McCarthy? McCarthyism? The McCarthy era?" Like most people, I thought McCarthy invented the Hollywood witch hunts, but the HUAC Hollywood trials started in 1947 and McCarthy didn't even get elected until 1950. He was also a Senator, not a Representative, so he wasn't in the House and he couldn't have served on HUAC. That is the nugget of information that most people don't realize.

Anyway, most of those guys you call commies were as American as apple pie. They fought in the war and wrote patriotic movies."

"Sure, but they were brainwashed by party propaganda, right? I read about one guy, Bernstein, who said that they *did* try to put commie messages into their scripts."

"Who said they did?"

"He did, in his own biography. Where do you get your information? Have you actually interviewed a live human about Thomas?"

"I don't like doing interviews. People say I'm confrontational."

"Now there's a shock."

I got up and walked to the rail. I liked to lean on it and watch the tankers in the harbor. I got comfortable and figured Phoebe would probably be gone when I turned around. Three Lucky Strikes later I turned to see I had been right.

It was the first time I had been right about her since I met her.

CHAPTER SEVEN
Trust Me

Staring at my typewriter, I considered writing about what had happened to me that day, and then deep-sixed that idea in favor of having another beer. Of course, it seemed criminal to let that poor beer drink alone so we invited Mr. Jack Daniels to the party. After a couple of hours I was on the balcony, plastered. I wondered if I might have imagined the whole thing in my drunken stupor. I had never before had hallucinations, but I guess there's a first time for everything. Anyway, I wasn't sure what had been real. Then I was leaning against the rail, feeling no pain when I suddenly realized I had a problem.

I was having trouble focusing, which wasn't unusual, and I was dizzy, which was also less-than-surprising, but I quickly realized that this problem was a bit more serious. In fact, I was no longer on the *safe-on-my-balcony* side of the rail. Instead, I was dangling on the *ten-stories-above-the-sidewalk-with-nothing-between-me-and-certain-death* side of the rail. Not only that, I was upside down.

I was hanging by my ankles with a beautiful view.

Surprisingly, I didn't panic. I was probably too drunk to realize the magnitude of my problem. Someone or something was holding on to me by my ankles, shins and feet. More accurately, it felt like a lot of hands were holding me, and my inverted perspective seemed to be increasing my stupor.

The Pacific Ocean and the Queen Mary were now upside down, but the view was still fabulous. Then, I heard what sounded like Munchkins arguing with each other and I was yanked around to face the building. My downstairs neighbors were making love in front of their fake fireplace, and in spite of my peril I was captivated by their progress. Then, just as things got interesting, I was yanked back around to my ocean view and the hands that held me started pulling me up.

I had gotten used to dangling, but once I started going up the ride became bumpy. I was banging against the building, and that hurt, even in my anesthetized state. Plus, I seemed to slip back a few times. It was as though all of the hands that held me were having trouble working in unison. From my perspective, I would rise up a few inches only to slip back down the same amount of space. While the blood rushed to my head the Queen Mary would lower and then rise and then the process would be repeated.

By this point, the Munchkin sounds from my balcony included grunting and groaning, but I didn't seem to be getting anywhere. I was mostly just banging against the building. Then I heard some weird noises, and a slightly more normal voice yelled, "Get back to work." After that, it felt like many more hands joined in to lift me. I thought I must have been dreaming when I heard the little voices shouting "heave," followed quickly by, "ho," and repeated the process again and again. I was anxious to find out what it was all about, but I blacked out before I made it to the top.

Then I had a bad dream.

A really bad dream.

It was a dream I had had many times before.

I was back in Afghanistan, and my unit was pinned down by a 50-calibre sniper and bombs were going off all around us. We were in the middle of a residential street lined with cars, and our Humvees were our only cover from the incoming artillery. The whole scene seemed to be moving in fast motion, and the only sound any of us could hear was ringing in our ears caused by the explosions.

The sniper crew that was attacking us was located on the top floor of a two story apartment building, and our convoy had been stopped when the lead vehicle was blown up by a mine planted in the street. It's a common form of ambush, and this was a textbook example from the Al Qaeda playbook. It works because the Insurgents hide among women and children and don't care how many innocents they kill. They make it impossible to kill them without killing the kids and women they are using for shields, and then they call us barbarians. We look bad to the world if we even defend ourselves. Nazis look like Candy Stripers compared to these punks.

The nose of the 50-cal stuck out of what had once been a picture window in someone's living room. Most of these countries had possibilities before the fascists took over. They had parks and hotels and restaurants. Now all they had was rubble and hatred. I wondered why the citizens of this country could allow these fascists to destroy their peaceful lives and civilization.

My two best friends, Harvey and Frank were pinned down on either side of me, and Colonel Dunbar was two cars ahead of me. Suddenly, the Colonel's Hummer got hit and I couldn't see him. Then Harvey took a hit from the 50-cal. His head exploded right off of his shoulders and the rest of him dropped like a rag doll. Then the Humvee that Frank was hiding behind exploded and all that was left was a crater about twice the size of the Hummer. Everything was moving too fast, and I figured I only had about five seconds to live, so I decided to climb out on a ledge like I always did.

I cocked my M-16 and checked to make sure I had the two grenades I always strapped to my vest, then I jumped out of the Humvee and ran straight for the apartment building. I wanted to make it quick, so I ran straight at the 50-cal. I didn't expect to make it, but waiting to die is boring.

By this time, the ground all around me was disappearing because explosions were going off to my right, left, front and back. I knew that one would hit me any moment and I would be finished, but I figured I might as well keep running while I still had two perfectly good grenades.

I noticed a little kid, maybe eight years old suddenly running after me. He was wearing an explosive vest and holding a detonator that was attached by a wire. He was screaming something, but I couldn't hear a thing over the ringing in my ears. Meanwhile, I was a lot faster than he was, and I continued running straight toward my objective. I looked up to see the picture window with the barrel of the 50-cal pointed at me and blazing, but somehow only hitting everything around me.

I wondered what was wrong with the shooter. I was literally staring right down the barrel of that gun, and although my comrades were dying on the right and left, it wasn't hitting me.

I turned back to see the little kid running, but an explosion opened up a crater right in front of him. When he stepped into it, he lost his footing and fell forward. He landed face first and the vest detonated. I could feel some shrapnel hit me from behind, but most of the damage was probably done to the walls of the crater. Then I saw a beautiful sight that took my mind off the horror behind me.

A large panel truck was parked next to the second floor balcony, probably to help these killers escape, but I had another goal for it. Without breaking stride, I jumped onto the hood of a car parked next to the truck and used it as a launching pad to jump onto the hood of the truck. Next, I jumped onto the roof of the truck and made a quick leap onto the fire escape at the side of the building.

The 50-cal shells exploded all around me, but somehow I hadn't been hit yet, so I kept going. Then a funny thing happened; I started laughing. For some reason, it was hilarious to me that they couldn't seem to hit me, and the faster I ran, the louder I seemed to laugh. I quickly used the fire escape to reach the roof, but the snipers knew I was up there, so they started shooting through the ceiling and holes suddenly opened up all around my feet. Since I hadn't yet been hit, I dove for the edge of the roof over the picture window and lobbed a grenade into the apartment.

Suddenly, all of the shooting stopped; all explosions stopped, and the only sounds I heard were Afghan screams (I couldn't tell if they were Pashto or Dari, but I could tell they were panicking.). I knew I was probably going to blow up any second, so I made a mad dash and leaped off the edge of the roof, bounded once off of the truck, and rolled back under it for cover.

That's when I heard my grenade in the apartment explode. They must have had some more explosives in the apartment because the horizon was filled with explosive clouds and shrapnel. The explosions continued for quite a while and then everything got quiet. At least as quiet as it could be with the massive ringing in my ears. I just laid under the truck for a while, and watched the dust slowly begin to settle all around me.

When I climbed out from under the truck, the Colonel had a few surviving insurgents in tie wrap, and the medics were attending to some of our wounded. When the Colonel saw me he just smiled and shook his head. I wandered over to where Frankie and Harvey had died. I was a little surprised to realize how much it hurt to lose those guys, and told myself I would never let that happen again.

When I woke up from my dream, I was lying on the floor of my balcony in Long Beach with chocolate pudding inside my head. My first thought was that I was still in Afghanistan, but I realized I had been dreaming when I felt the cool breeze coming off of the Pacific.

Everything was fuzzy when my vision started to come back, and then I noticed someone standing over me. He looked like a little old man, but he smelled like sulfur. At first I didn't think too much about it, but there was something familiar about this old man that I couldn't place. Once he came into focus, I realized this was not just any old man; it was J. Parnell Thomas himself.

I recognized him from the pictures at the Nix, and it's a good thing I was so drunk, because this experience would probably have killed a sober man. I tried to ask him if he was real, but he got fuzzy again and faded to black. I guess I passed out again.

When I woke up the next time, I was still lying on the balcony, but J. Parnell was sitting on my couch, watching my 64-inch flat screen, which surprised me, because I sure hadn't paid the cable bill. A 7-Eleven commercial came on and everyone on TV was drinking Slurpees. As always, these TV people were completely refreshed by the frosty frozen beverage, and it made me want one. I was, by this time, leaning up on my elbows, trying to determine whether or not I was dreaming. The old man suddenly got very agitated. He squirmed and danced like he had to pee, then turned, saw I was awake, and leaped to his feet pointing frantically at the commercial.

"You gotta get me one of those."

"I gotta?"

"Get me a red one, no a purple one, and make it snappy."

"Wait a minute."

"Wait nuthin'. Get me one of those and we'll talk."

"But I..."

I struggled to get up off the floor while Thomas folded his arms over his chest and sat like Buddha on the couch. He was obviously not going to be good company until I got him a Slurpee, but I ached all over and was pretty sure I had a concussion. I was also trying to determine if I had already gone insane, or was still on the pathway to insanity.

"Okay, so you're claiming, you woke up and found out you were dreaming, right?"

"If you recall, I said you wouldn't believe me."

"So you're saying a real-life-dead-Congressman pulled you up over the tenth floor balcony, saving you from certain death, and then told you to run out and get him a Slurpee?"

"I will admit, when you say it like that, it sounds pretty farfetched."

"You think?"

"Now shut up or book me, because this is the only way I know how to tell it."

J. Parnell was mesmerized by my TV.

"Wow, you get great reception with this thing. Where are the bunny ears?"

I decided to avoid explaining the whole technological revolution.

"Are you who I think you are?"

"Yes I am."

"So what are you doing in my living room?"

"I heard you were looking for me. Now get me a whatchamcalit before I change my mind."

"Wait a minute. I'm not going to..."

I had done something wrong there, and I knew it.

J. Parnell turned to face me, but the jovial little elf had disappeared and his eyes glowed like fireballs. I decided to stop arguing because he looked like he had been created for a horror movie. But before I could do as he wished, he reached over and put his hand on top of mine. I didn't know what he did, but I would fight long and hard before I let him do it again. His touch made me feel like all the bones in my body switched places.

It was a new kind of pain, and when he let go of me, I yearned to cling to the fragile source of life inside me. I was no longer a smart guy, I was scared, and I figured I better do what he said.

I left him in the apartment while I limped off for a Slurpee. There's a 7-Eleven on Pine, so I was back in under ten minutes. When I came in my front door, the old man was nowhere to be seen, and I felt secure in the knowledge that I had been hallucinating. In fact, I was comforted by the knowledge that I had not actually gotten involved with a demon from hell. I was so glad to just be crazy and not demon possessed. I didn't believe in that stuff, but why tempt fate?

Suddenly, the little weasel popped up from behind my kitchen counter like a deranged jack in the box, stopping my heart and ruining my nice secure feeling.

"What took you so long?"

He couldn't have been much more than five feet tall, and he wasn't exactly in good shape. His skin was weathered even worse than my publisher's and his black suit was filthy and wrinkled, with burn holes interrupting the pin stripes every few inches. He wore a shirt that had probably been white once, but now it was the color of café au lait with chocolate sprinkles. His crowning glory was a rotten egg smell that I doubted I would ever get out of my couch.

Neither of us bothered with conversation, and J. Parnell made a grab for the frosty beverage.

"Gimmee!"

He stood holding the Slurpee for a moment, and smiled, revealing a few rotten teeth amid a wide expanse of rotting gums and other nasty visuals. He held the beverage to his cheek and sighed like a little girl. Then he took off the plastic top and poured some of the icy purple goo slowly into his pants.

"Aah!"

The pinched, ugly look on his face quickly changed to a pinched, satisfied look. He gummed his lower lip and crossed his eyes, his smile grew wider, which was frankly hard to take, and he sat holding the cup like a baby holds a teddy bear. He would occasionally take a tiny sip from the top of the cup, and react with glee.

"Oh, my dark lord that's good. Oooh that's good! So good. That's good. That's real good."

Then he would take another tiny sip and repeat the performance.

"Oooooooooh that's goooooooooood! That's sooooooooo gooooooooooood!"

I was starting to get tired of his antics, but I knew something he didn't.

"Oh baby that's good. That's goody-good-goo, AAAH!"

He suddenly stopped and smacked his palm against his forehead as though he suddenly realized he had forgotten something. Then he contorted his face like he was in silent movies. He grabbed his face with both hands; he was in agony and didn't know how to handle it.

"We call that a brain freeze."

"Aaagh! You could warn a fella you know."

"Okay dude, tell me what this is all about."

"Simple, I...aaagh"

He slammed his palm against his forehead again.

"Fudge, that hurts! What?"

"I said, what's this all about?"

"Simple, you need a book and I need a legacy."

"So you expect me to believe you are really a ghost?"

"I suppose I am in the conventional sense, but technically, I'm a soul; a soul who has returned."

"And why am I so lucky?"

He turned and smiled with an evil twinkle in his eyes.

"You're right to assume that there's a catch."

Then he pulled out a legal document and a golden fountain pen. I took the document and gave it a look.

"A contract for my immortal soul?"

"Right, you don't believe in all that hoodoo anyway, so we can easily make a deal tonight."

"But if there's really a hell, then there's got to be a heaven, right? And if there's a heaven, there's a God."

"If there were really a God, would you have been dragged into Father Seamus's office every week for all those years?"

"Wait a minute." Detective Jones interrupted. "What's all this about Father Seamus?"

"It's nothing."

"Don't give me that."

I just sat staring at Detective Jones for a while, but I finally decided to talk.

"I wasn't going to tell you. Truth is I've never told anybody."

"You don't have to. I can do the math. You're telling me you were one of the statistics everybody hears about, right?"

It took a while, but I nodded.

"When I lived at the orphanage I was an Altar Boy, and one of the priests put a little too much effort into his work."

"And J. Parnell knew about it?"

"Yeah. That's when I started to get nervous."

"*That's* when you started to get nervous? The part before this didn't make you nervous? I'm nervous and I wasn't even there. What happened next?"

"I guess he knew my weak spot, because I wanted to tell him to shove it, then suddenly I wanted to sign the stupid contract. But I still had enough scrutiny to bargain."

"What do I get in return?"

"You get me, J. Parnell Thomas, Republican, New Jersey; Chairman of the House Un-American Activities Committee. I assume you noticed that it's hard to get much information about me. Sign this paper and you get first hand details on the Communist scare by the guy who made it all happen."

"Seems to me you get something too, since McCarthy is getting credit for everything you did."

As soon as I said it I knew it was a mistake. His eyes narrowed and his jaw tightened. The next thing I knew, J. Parnell exploded into a rage, pulled out a big gavel and started banging it on all the furniture.

Kerblam went the gavel as he slammed it down on a chair and reduced it to splinters.

"You are out of order, sir. You are out of order! I demand order in these proceedings!"

The head of the gavel was solid oak. It was at least a foot long and six inches in diameter. It took both hands for him to wield it. This was a weapon that could do some serious damage.

"That son-of-a-buck McCarthy stole my thunder. All those books should have been about me! All those movies should have been about me!"

Everything he hit with that gavel disintegrated, and every time he pounded it, sparks flew out like a muffler dragging on the highway. I think I even saw lightning. Pretty soon my whole apartment was full of sparklers, splinters and shrapnel. It looked like Lindsay Lohan's hotel room.

He kept banging the gavel until he finally busted the head off the stupid thing and it flew over the balcony. Then he suddenly calmed down, as though all the steam was out of him and he wasn't mad any more. From the street I could hear squealing tires and crushing metal and glass. I offered him a Lucky Strike and he took it, and then I fired up one for myself. Soon, we were both blowing smoke rings and relaxing.

"So how does the deal work?"

"I will meet you here for thirty minutes, every other day until the book is finished in two weeks."

"Wait a minute. Why every other day? And what makes you think I can finish a book in two weeks?"

Then he winked at me, which was the second time a man had winked at me and I still didn't like it, but he leaned in so close I could smell the sulphur on his breath.

"It's guaranteed to be a best-seller."

I will admit that the prospect of writing a best-selling book carries with it a tremendous appeal. As such, I was extremely interested in his proposal, but...

"Then I go to hell when I die?"

"Sure, just like your old man and all your friends. Father Seamus is there too. But you and I need to do one thing a little different."

Then the little gerbil held up a golden fountain pen. It was beautiful and I reached for it, but instead of handing it to me, he used it to stab me in the finger. Suddenly, I had a little pool of blood on my kitchen table.

"Ouch. What are you doing?"

"It must be signed in blood, just like in the horror movies."

He dipped the pen in the blood and handed it to me. The next thing I knew, my name appeared in red right next to a post-it that read, *sign here*. I was standing there, bleeding on my carpet, wondering what I had done, and what would follow.

"How do I know you'll live up to your end of the bargain?"

He stared at me with an evil grin.

"Trust me."

He took another sip of Slurpee and smiled with delight.

"Sorry about the thing on the balcony."

"Huh?"

"I'll tell you later."

"What?"

"I said I was sorry."

At that point, I once again started hoping I was dreaming, because this adventure was becoming a little too thrilling for me. I just stared at the little man for a minute.

"This is gonna end badly, isn't it?"

He displayed a disgusting smile and started cackling like a giant chicken. Then he began to disappear. Yes, I said disappear. Suddenly, everything except the Slurpee de-materialized and he vanished. The plastic cup of purple Slurpee seemed to hang in midair for a moment and then dropped to the floor, spilling all over the carpet.

I heard his voice echo, "Phooey!" from the spiritual realm. A little later I heard a knock at the door. When I opened it, you were on the other side.

"Wait just a minute Hemingway. Even if I believed any of this, and I don't, it doesn't explain how Melvin wound up mashed into your dryer."

"You know it's a funny thing. I didn't even know I had a dryer. I should really have been more attentive."

"Or maybe you were too attentive, to Melvin I mean, when you killed him. He was strangled, mangled and folded."

"And I had no idea that a fully grown man could be made to fit inside a residential Kenmore. Did you?"

"Skip that, and tell me how you did it."

"You're gonna have to wait to see how Melvin gets killed because it would spoil the surprise if I told you."

"Tell me."

"Nope. Throw me in the hoosegow if you don't like my process. I'm the director of this movie, and if I wanna jump back and forth in time like Quentin Tarantino, I'll do it."

"You are really pushing my buttons, Hemingway."

"Are you ready to listen to the story my way?"

"Make it good, because I'm losing interest."

"No you aren't. You remember what happened when you came into my apartment?"

"Sure, we found Melvin's body in your clothes dryer, I arrested you and you gave me the slip."

"Right, I knew how to get out of handcuffs. Your guys should have gotten them on tighter."

"Yeah-yeah-yeah, we know you got away, but what happened next?"

CHAPTER EIGHT
Softly and Tenderly

Before you showed up I found myself taking another nap.

I remembered J. Parnell's disappearing act, and then I was asleep. I was listening to something like the ocean, but I knew it wasn't that. We can't hear waves in Long Beach because of the breakwater. As I woke up, the noises got louder and weirder. I used all my strength to get my eyes open, and then I was sorry I did, because everything was sideways. I figured out I was lying on the carpet surrounded by a whole lotta purple, and realized I was smack in the middle of a puddle of icy purple glop, like a Slurpee-carrying tanker had run aground on my face, which was now lying sideways in the no-longer-delicious frozen treat. The enormous, economy-sized cup was acting like a seashell, creating ocean sounds, and the icy sludge was oozing into my ear.

Every part of my body hurt. I staggered to my feet like an old man and headed for the icebox. I spotted a big envelope with J. Parnell's contract on my kitchen table. S*eller's copy* was written in big letters across the top of the page. Then I looked around and noticed the shambles my apartment had become. I had to get out of there.

"Except I heard a knock and then you and your pals came in."

"Why did you let us in with a body in the dryer?"

"I didn't know there was a body in the dryer. Suddenly, I was in handcuffs. How did you even know to come to my apartment?

"That's classified. How did you get out of the handcuffs?"

Well, one of the tricks I learned at the orphanage was to get myself out of handcuffs. Pushing down on a little lever with some kind of probe will snap the cuffs open. It's easy if you know how. I was palming a paper clip from the contract when they locked me up and I had the cuffs unlocked before they started rolling out the crime scene tape.

They left me standing there alone when everyone ran into the laundry room to check out Melvin. I didn't know why they did, but I took advantage of the situation and strolled into the hallway. There was only one copper guarding the door. I put that guy to sleep with one punch and grabbed the envelope that J. Parnell had left on the table. I probably cleared the lobby before they even knew I was gone.

Next thing I knew, I was on the street heading for who-knows-where? I averted my eyes when I saw a small accident that was the result of a fifteen pound gavel head had that caved in the roof of a Honda Accord on the street below my window. Fortunately, it had not come down on the driver's side or the damage might have been worse. I averted my eyes a second time as I passed 7-Eleven just in case J. Parnell was ordering another Slurpee, and then I hailed a cab to take me to the Rock Bottom, but I couldn't get a cab to stop. Every driver took one look at me and kept driving. I couldn't figure out what was happening until I scratched my head and felt the sticky glop in my hair. I didn't realize it, but I was still wearing my crap from the night before, my hair was a spiky, purple, punk rock nightmare, and I was standing in front of a homeless blind guy playing *Softly and Tenderly Jesus is Calling* on a busted guitar.

"Softly and tenderly, Jesus is calling, calling for you and for me."

Like me, he was dirty, but unlike me, he had a beautiful singing voice.

"See on the portals he's waiting and watching, watching for you and for me."

He looked like Isaac Hayes, except his eyes seemed to be looking in different directions. One eye stared off into the distance, but the other one was staring right at me, and creeping me out.

"Come home, come home; ye who are weary come home."

He had a sign around his neck that read, BLIND, and virtually every inch of this dude's clothes was covered in patches. It was as if the original material was completely gone and all that was left was the patches.

"Earnestly, tenderly, Jesus is calling, calling, Oh sinner, come home."

I wondered if he was a faker, because I stood there looking at him and he stood there looking back at me, neither of us saying a word.

Then a funny thing happened: Patches stopped playing. He rose up and pointed his finger at me like he was picking me out of a lineup. If he really was blind, he was doing a good imitation of a sighted guy. He held his blind cane in one hand and with the other he wiggled a crooked finger at me and shouted, "COME TO ME, ALL YE WHO ARE WEAK AND HEAVY-LADEN, AND I WILL GIVE YOU REST." His voice was raspy, yet somehow booming. Like a cross between Jessie Jackson and Harvey Feirstein. Everyone walking by on the street turned and looked at me like I stole his watch. Then he said it again, "COME TO ME, ALL YE WHO ARE WEAK AND HEAVY-LADEN, AND I WILL GIVE YOU REST."

I couldn't move. Patches was pointing at me and I couldn't move. That was all I needed.

"Okay, so what? Who cares what a homeless guy said?"

"Interrupting."

"Loser."

"You want me to stop? Because I'm ready for a nap in a nice warm cell."

"You don't have to get nasty."

As I was saying, I got away from Patches and started hustling down the sidewalk. Then I remembered I couldn't go anywhere looking like I did, and I couldn't go back upstairs. I finally got a cab to stop, probably because the driver's hair was as purple as mine. I spotted you and your boys rolling out of the lobby door as we were pulling away from the scene of the crime.

Down the street from the Rock Bottom was a men's store that was plastered with *Going out of Business* banners. I had been told that the store had been going out of business since 1971. I had never been in the store, but the Slurpee-encrusted outfit I was wearing was making my life difficult, so I had the cabbie drop me off in front.

Although most of the men passing by the store wore jeans and sneakers, this store specialized in men's suits, and when I walked in I was taken with all of the mannequins wearing suits of various colors. I had no interest in one of the delicate-looking business suits and turned to leave. A salesman spotted me and walked me back into the store like he was escorting me to the prom.

"How can I fulfill your sartorial goals to-day?"

The guy was short, smelled like too much *Brut* and had his patter down to a science. Exactly the type of dude I generally avoid.

"I'm just looking."

But this guy wasn't going to take no for an answer. He actually put his finger up in the air and shooshed me as though he was calming a hysterical child.

"You don't have to worry any more. I am here to make all these sticky clothes a bad memory."

I was used to fighting my way out of ugly situations, but I didn't quite know what to do with this guy. I waited to see what he had in mind and he escorted me into the back room where several old Jews sat in a dimly-lit room cutting suits. My new pal escorted me past them to a collection of rolling racks filled with suits. Finally, he pulled the last rack aside to reveal a slightly dusty mannequin in a black suit and white shirt combination that perfectly captured the *Blues Brothers* look.

He took it off of the mannequin and handed it to me. Without further words, he pointed me to a dressing room and I found myself following direction. The next thing I knew I was clean and shiny in a black suit and white shirt that fit as though it had been built specifically for me. Everything from my Slurpee-covered shoes to my Slurpee-soaked underwear had been replaced. The salesman helped me to create a perfect slipknot and sent me on my way. I left my old clothes in a trash can next to the Jews.

The cabbie dropped me off at Rock Bottom and I took my time walking in. I looked and felt quite different than the night before. After a quick Red Pelican, I went out front to grab another cab, but when I got there, Patches was singing in front of the restaurant patio. I might have looked different, but the blind man knew me immediately.

He kept singing *Softly and Tenderly* without turning in my direction, but when I passed in front of him he said, "You can run, but you can't hide." His voice was soft and low and convincing. I didn't even slow down. I hustled to the nearest cab and jumped in.

I opened the envelope that J. Parnell had left and a big pile of hundred dollar bills fell out. They were a little bit singed around the edges, but looked real; fifty thousand dollars worth of real. There was also an invoice for six months' rent on my place that was stamped, "paid in full," which was pretty surprising because I sure hadn't paid it. However, I didn't have time to worry about such petty developments.

Maybe things were back on the upswing, I thought. Maybe I could take care of business and get this whole ugly episode behind me. I told myself not to think about what had happened that last night.

"Did it work?"

"Like Viet Nam."

I told my driver to take me back to the Nix.

"Wait a minute. You were on the lam for a murder rap and you hid out in the Richard Nixon Library?"

"When was the last time you heard of a killer being caught in a presidential archive?"

"Good point. Next time, I'm looking there first."

On the way to the Nix, I couldn't help wondering what kind of crap I had fallen into. I knew I would never get another chance as a writer unless I made a splash with this biography. If I did, maybe I could get back to writing the bad stories I really wanted to tell.

Of course, I would have to live through this book to write another one.

The driver dropped me off at the Nix by the big fountain and I handed him two slightly singed hundreds. I made my way up the steps, but Edyth was suddenly standing in front of me, dressed like an extra-husky Gloria Swanson. She wore enormous round sunglasses, a hat that could have provided shade for a sport utility vehicle, and all the leathery skin she had proudly displayed before was now covered with mounds of fluffy scarves. She looked like a leather chew toy sitting on top of a banana split.

"Joe darling, you haven't returned my calls."

"Lady I don't even have a phone."

"But of course you do my love."

Suddenly, I heard a ringing sound inside my pocket. I reached in and pulled out a cell phone with a tiny little TV screen. I opened it up and Edyth's face was on the TV. She said, "Answer my calls from now on or there will be serious consequences." Then I looked up and she was gone, so I headed for the front door. Passing a big trashcan that looked practically sterile, the phone started to ring, and I tossed it into the dumper with a clank.

Inside, I rode down in the elevator with Nancy the Nazi and got back to work on the scrapbook. The work was slow, challenging, and fascinating, but it was hard to get a real picture of who the man was. After about an hour, Nancy the Nazi wandered off and I stood up to stretch. I turned around and found Edyth with a hungry look on her face. She grabbed me again, yanked me close and gave me a very painful hickey. She seemed to have the strength of ten men, and she was sucking on my neck so hard that it felt like I was being forcibly fondled by the world's largest Hoover. I finally broke free, or at least I thought I did, because she disappeared before I could compose myself. I knew I was a mess, red-faced and wrinkled when the Nazi returned, but I didn't realize I had a hickey on my neck the size of Rhode Island.

"It's noon. You must leave for one hour," she told me.

"Right." I was completely out of snappy banter. Then my jacket pocket started ringing again. I reached inside and found the phone I had previously tossed, and once again, Edyth's face was on the screen making kissy faces.

"I warned you my dear. You will now understand the consequences of your actions. Please don't make us do this again."

That was a threat. What did she mean by it? Did she think I was concerned about my safety? It turned out that she knew something I didn't.

Outside, I started to dodge traffic on Imperial, heading toward a promising looking deli across the street, but once I was committed, I noticed Phoebe crossing in the other direction. When she saw me she stopped in the center of the street. She started to turn around and go back, when all of a sudden, a big black Hummer changed lanes and started roaring toward her.

Edyth knew that I wouldn't be concerned about my own safety, but I would be very concerned about Phoebe's. Frankly I was surprised by the degree of my concern as I ran to try and do something.

The windows of the Hummer were completely blacked out so you couldn't see who was driving, and the big SUV was flying down the road by the time Phoebe saw it. I expected her to run, or jump, or something, but instead she turned and looked at me.

Why would she do that?

My stomach rode the elevator between nausea and hysteria and I could see the Hummer was right on top of her. I was running as fast as I could. I didn't have any hope of getting to her, and even less chance of being able to save her, but I ran like never before. By this time, the Hummer was probably doing eighty, and Phoebe was looking at me like she knew something I didn't.

"What happened?"

I looked past her to the other side of the street and saw Patches standing there, which would have freaked me out if I hadn't already been so freaked out.

Patches didn't have his guitar. He had his arms stretched out from his sides, and he was holding his blind cane like a staff; as though he was Charlton Heston parting the Red Sea. He looked like he was praying, but all I could hear was traffic. I could see the Hummer was right on top of Phoebe, and I was about ten feet away when it happened.

"What happened?"

The Hummer passed right through her.

"Huh?"

"You heard me, it passed right through her."

"How?"

"How do I know how? If I had to guess, I would say it's the same stuff that Chuck Heston used on the Red Sea."

Then Patches wiggled his big crooked finger at me said something I couldn't hear because of the traffic, but I would bet money it was the "weak and heavy laden" routine, whatever that means.

Then I remembered the creep in the Hummer had just tried to kill Phoebe. I was still in the street, so I flagged down a car to chase the Hummer. I spotted a nice Crown Victoria, which is a highly underrated vehicle for this sort of thing.

"You will get no argument from me."

Anyway, the Crown Vic also had blacked out windows, so I couldn't see inside. I stood in front of it and it stopped, then the passenger door swung open. When I got in, I saw the reason why. It was Leo, and he was holding a gun on me, and he was agitated that he hadn't been able to find Melvin.

"You really couldn't blame him for being upset."

I wanted to chase the Hummer, but Leo wanted to argue about a payment plan. Then, I realized I had suddenly started to feel better.

"Better?"

"Yeah. I suddenly realized that all this weirdness had thrown me off my game. I had been completely out of my element. Everywhere I went, I was the visiting team, but when Leo tried to get tough with me, I was suddenly back in the middle of my smelly, rat-infested home field, and I was finally hungry for hitting."

Leo pointed his gun at me, and without hesitating, I grabbed it and shoved it into his face. I repeated the process a few times and started breaking up his dental work. Then I took the Roscoe and smacked him across the temple so hard I probably could have quit right there, but the little weasel managed to threaten me one more time.

"You are a dead man."

So I opened his driver's door, which changed his mood completely.

"I was just kidding. I didn't mean it. Take the car. Take the gun. Take my Visa card."

I shoved him out into traffic and turned my attention to the fleeing Hummer. I was exhilarated by the tussle and I would ordinarily have prolonged it a little longer, but I had to deal with the creep who just tried to kill Phoebe.

I zipped through traffic like a NASCAR driver. Before I knew it I was right on the Hummer's butt and starting to enjoy myself. I pulled into position to do that cop maneuver where they spin the car they're chasing. I had never done it, but how hard could it be? I got my front end right next to the Hummer's rear and hammered a hard left turn into the back end. I didn't know if it would work, but the Crown Vic packed quite a wallop and the big fella spun around a few times before it started rolling. It rolled over and over across Imperial Highway, down an embankment, and then it got launched over a backyard fence by a beautifully-landscaped sloping lawn. It flew through the air and landed on its roof in the middle of a well-tended swimming pool.

I pulled over, hopped the fence, and ran toward the scene. The Hummer was sinking fast, and I noticed these squirrelly little guys climbing out of it. They didn't look tough. In fact, they looked kinda like refugees from a prison camp; a prison camp for cartoon munchkins. But they all looked the same, like brothers, twin brothers, except that there were five or six of them.

"They would be sextuplets."

"Thank you so much for your contribution."

They all looked like that old-time character actor whose name I couldn't remember. He was in all those gangster movies. You know the guy that said, "Okay you guys…"

"Jimmy Cagney?"

"No, he said, 'Is this the end of Rico?'"

"Oh, yeah, what was that guy's name?"

Anyway, they were each about four feet tall, but they didn't look like dwarves, they looked like a cartoon version of that actor, whatsisname. They had a disgusting, greenish skin tone that was set off by bright red eyes. And they blinked a lot, which was a little hard to take with those big red eyes.

But their most disturbing feature was a scar each Blinker had across his face. The scars started on each one's left cheek and looked like Edward Scissorhands had slapped him across the mouth. Four, blood-encrusted grooves dragged across the meaty part of each Blinker's face, and those faces were pretty crusty to begin with. I was very frustrated that I couldn't remember that actor's name, but figured I better address the ugly little Blinkers coming toward me.

They squawked at each other while the Hummer slowly submerged. Their voices sounded like the noise you get when you fast-forward audio tape, or the sound the Munchkins made in *The Wizard of Oz*. Except these guys weren't talking about lollipops. I heard words that sounded like "kill," "stab" and "eat."

"Edward G. Robinson."

"What?"

"It was Edward G. Robinson. The actor who said, 'Is this the end of Rico'?"

Right. Anyway, they were coming at me from all sides, so I figured I better stop thinking and start hitting. I grabbed one by the shoulders and he just went limp. I let go and he fell to the ground and rolled into a ball. Then they all went limp and rolled into balls, like possums. They were playing possum. They were, that is, until I started to pick one up. The little creep hissed and showed me some fangs the size of a lawn mower.

Not teeth, fangs.

They all had 'em, and suddenly, they were coming after me with those huge fangs and a big ugly hissing noise. I grabbed a wrought iron deck chair and smacked the first one with it. It knocked him about ten feet through the air. Then he started jumping around the deck squealing like a dog. Then he blew up.

"He blew up, as in he got angry?"

"No, he blew up as in there was a violent expansion of molecules, and his disgusting green body spewed green glop all over the neighborhood."

"That is different."

"Welcome to my world."

I stood there and watched the next one start shaking like a break dancer, then he made these really weird noises and smells, and then he exploded into a cloud of purple glop, which came raining down all over me, the pool, everything. Then the other four guys all exploded too. Boom, boom, boom, boom. Glop, glop, glop, glop. A nice little house in Yorba Linda was suddenly a location shoot for *The Exorcist*.

I didn't want to hang around waiting for the cops, and I wanted to check on Phoebe, so I hopped into the Crown Vic and started back.

By the time I got back to the scene of the original crime, Phoebe and Patches were both gone, and by the time I got home that night, I had re-programmed all the radio channels on my new Crown Victoria. I pulled it into the space where I used to park the Lexus, and some jerk with a Mercedes had parked a foot over the line into my space.

"I hate that."

"Tell me about it. Why can't they make a tougher law for the losers who do that?

"If it were up to me."

"I decided not to take it, so I used my new Crown Vic to gently push his car back where it belonged."

"Gently?"

"Well, now that I think of it, I was probably pretty stern."

"Oh MAN, I would love to do that."

"It was pretty cool."

"Did you do much damage?"

"Just to *his* car; the Crown Vic was barely scratched."

"Oh, YEAH that's great."

Then I noticed that the street was filled with police cars. I decided I needed another place to lay low.

CHAPTER NINE
Sasquatch and Starchy Potatoes

The Crown Vic made the ride to Newport Beach a bit more comfortable, and a radio interview with Vince Gilligan made the time pass quickly. I checked into a nondescript hotel because I assumed it would be a good spot to hide. The cops had no reason to look for me in Newport, and I like the way the beach smells.

Newport is a great beach that always seems comfortable. No one ever seems to work there; only surf, bike and consume copious amounts of food and drink. It seems like the people who grew up there are all blonde, tanned and happy, and the people who moved there as adults are just happy.

The clerk at the hotel scrutinized the burn marks on the bills, but they passed the all-important *yellow highlighter test*, so the dude welcomed me with open arms. I was starving, and I was right across the street from my favorite joint in Newport. Fortunately, it's easy to get lost in a place like *The Crab Cooker*, where fat cats and surf bums dine side by side on paper plates.

It took a while to get in. There is always a line of people hungry for shrimp. I finished off a plate of the famous grilled shrimp with extra-starchy potatoes, and then wandered down the street to *Thumpers*, one of the few real dives left in that part of town. In this dive, the surf bums would be overdressed, but I always seem to be able to think better amid the peace and quiet of a noisy bar with a scratchy jukebox. Don't ask me why.

I took one look at the bartender's dishrag and knew not to ask for a glass. Once I was relaxing behind a bottle of Newcastle I replayed the events of the past 48 hours. But no matter how many I drank, I couldn't get my story to make sense. Where I come from people don't blow up, or disappear into the spirit realm, and prior to this I had never known anyone to sell his or her soul to the devil.

When I got back to the hotel, I was feeling a buzz from the brown ale, but not too drunk to notice Leo sitting in a car in the parking lot. I have to say I was surprised that he had been able to find me. What were the odds that this hood had Lo-Jack? I was also impressed that he was able to survive the fall from his car after I shoved him out into traffic.

But he was a mess, sitting in the front seat of a brand new Crown Vic, he was bandaged, seemingly from head to toe. He had one of those casts where his arm was elevated by a pole from his midsection, making it look like he was permanently resting his elbow on thin air. His jaw was wired shut, he had two black eyes on top of a broken nose and a big cushion wrapped around his neck. He sat there smoking, and staring at the door to my room.

I took out the Colt 45 I had confiscated from him earlier. I knew he wouldn't come alone, and I also knew that if he returned to Dimitrios without the money or my head, Uncle Max would have him whacked.

Since I was dealing with bigger issues than this little weasel, I had figured a way out of this without either of us dying. I decided to buy my way out. I snuck around behind the car and cocked the Colt right behind Leo's ear.

"Don't shoot. I'll give you everything I got."

"I don't know, Leo. What have you got?"

"Is that you, McCoy? I'm not here for you, honest."

I reached into his coat and removed a Colt that was identical to the one at his ear. I've got to hand it to Leo; the man was a stickler for brand loyalty.

"Come on, Leo, I know you have to come back with the dough, so tell me what it takes to make our little problem go away."

"Okay, your ten grand, plus ten grand more for Melvin."

"Ten grand? That guy's not worth ten cents. I heard that Max was about to whack Melvin himself."

"Yeah, but you made him testy when you killed him without permission."

"I didn't... Never mind. You are telling me that if I make good on the debt *and* the fine, our problem goes away?"

"Completely, but how you gonna do that?"

I peeled off two-hundred of the singed century notes and counted them out for Leo. He held out his one good hand, but I stopped and pulled back.

"Call off your dogs."

He gave me an innocent look.

"I didn't bring anyone with me."

"Leo, I have two guns and no tolerance for your crap."

Leo lowered his eyes, then finally leaned over and flashed his headlights twice. Slowly, two guys in Two-Eleven Suits emerged from hiding spaces around my front door. They were both twenty-ish and whiter-than-white. The two *couldn't-have-been-more-white* dudes each wore a *turned-sideways* baseball cap and large gold chains. The would-be gangsters looked moronic, and in this case, looks were probably not deceiving. While keeping my gun on Leo, I pointed Leo's Colt at them.

"Put your roscoes on the hood of the car."

They looked at Leo, who nodded, then winced from the pain in his neck, and they reluctantly placed their pistols on the car. I wiggled the Colt at them and after a little shrugging; they placed their backup guns on the hood as well. I looked around, then I looked in the back seat of the Crown Vic, and then I looked at Leo.

"What?"

I re-cocked the Colt right between his eyes.

"Okay-okay-okay. Tony!"

I looked around the lot, and no Tony. I tapped the barrel of the Colt against Leo's skull. This made Leo very nervous.

"Ow, ow, ow. Tony, come on out," he yelled, "I'm not kidding."

Finally, the other two hoodlums joined in with the calling.

"Come on Tony, quit foolin' around."

Finally, a short, dark man in a burgundy Members Only jacket emerged from behind the dumpster. He made the long trek to the Crown Vic and deposited his two guns on the hood. Then he looked at Leo sweating under the barrel of his own Colt.

"I coulda had him."

I handed Leo the stack of bills and pushed a large trashcan over near the guns.

"Filler-up fellas."

"Aw, my girlfriend gave me that gun."

They grudgingly dumped their pieces in the can and climbed into the car as Leo counted the bills.

"I don't want to see you again, Leo."

"Yeah, yeah, whatever."

Tony started the car and they drove off down Pacific Coast Highway. I turned and walked back toward my room.

But I didn't go into my room.

Thirty minutes later the hotel was significantly darker when Leo's new Crown Vic came back. This time they didn't pull into the lot, but parked on the street as traffic whizzed by. Again, the three hoodlums got out of the car, only this time they all converged on room 13--my room.

They had new guns and they held them sideways, which gangsters do in movies, but in real life is no way to aim a weapon. They approached with stealth, if not grace, and when they got to the front door, they turned to each other in a clumsy whisper.

"Okay, on three we kick it in."

"So one-two-three, then we kick?"

"No, we kick on three."

"So one-two-kick?"

"Yeah."

"What about three?"

"Moron."

About this time, I got tired of waiting. I hadn't been in my room yet and I had to go to the bathroom really bad.

"Hey."

When I spoke, they all whirled with pistols blazing. The night became light with all of the shots that were being fired. Unfortunately for them, I was leaning behind a short concrete wall. These guys couldn't see too well, and they also couldn't shoot too well, but they could shoot a lot. When I heard three clicks, I knew their guns were empty. I jumped up and stood there holding Leo's two Colts.

"Bad shootin' Ringo."

They all three reached for their ankles, and came up with backup guns.

"No," I said, and the first two goons gave it up, but Members Only Tony grabbed his gun.

"Don't do it!"

107

But he wouldn't listen. I shot him in the middle of his forehead as the other two fell to the ground in surrender. I turned quickly to see Leo struggling to get out of his car with yet another Colt in his cast-encased right hand.

"Leo, stop."

But he didn't listen to me. He opened the door, put his good foot on the ground, and tripped over it with the bad one. He fell into oncoming traffic, right under a motor home headed toward Mexico.

Since I didn't hear any sirens, I turned back to the two goons in tracksuits.

"Into the room."

"Don't kill me man. It was just business."

"Don't kill me either, man. I'm in the same business he is."

"Move into the room before I start shooting."

They reluctantly got up and moved to the door. I gave one my room key and he opened it.

"Straight through to the bathroom, boys."

They moved with the enthusiasm of Auschwitz prisoners, but finally made it to the bathroom. I nodded for them to get into the shower. With some extended prodding, they did. They both looked like they were going to cry when I shut the shower door on them and turned on the water. Then I carefully put the Colt in my back pocket, unzipped my pants and started to pee. Man it felt good. I had been holding it way too long. I didn't want to give the losers time to think, so I quickly zipped and turned around.

I had underestimated my opposition.

I struggled to turn around because I wasn't finished peeing. I couldn't aim without peeing all over the floor, which, in retrospect doesn't seem like it would have been so horrible. Then I saw him. He was the size of a double-door refrigerator. His face had obviously stopped more than its share of fists, and he wore his hair in a long flat top with lots of butch wax. He wore a cheap black suit similar to mine with a sweaty white shirt underneath. His red tie made him look less like a killer and more like Rodney Dangerfield on steroids.

He stood holding a gun on me, although I wasn't sure he would have needed it, even if I started shooting. This dude was so big; he would have had to turn sideways to come through the door, so he motioned instead for me to come out to him.

He was the Sasquatch of button men.

He made a circular gesture with his gun and I took it to mean he wanted me to turn around. When I did, he removed Leo's Colt from my back pocket.

"Did Uncle Max send you?"

"Yeah."

"I paid off Leo."

"Yeah, but Mr. Dimitrios has other issues he wishes to discuss with you."

This was bad. I had always been able to work out a deal with the bookies, but Uncle Max wasn't going to be so easy. I had just passed the threshold into the room when Sasquatch raised his gun and fired twice. My ears exploded but I didn't seem to be hit. While a siren blared in my ears, I turned to see that the guys in the shower were not so lucky as blood and water came pouring out onto the shattered glass and all over the bathroom floor.

Sasquatch leaned toward his two fallen comrades as though they could still hear him.

"Mr. Dimitrios is displeased."

CHAPTER TEN
Uncle Max

Sasquatch held a gun on me while I drove his champagne-colored Coupe de Ville. He told me where to turn and how fast to go. Sitting next to me in the front seat, I couldn't help but notice that he also wore excessive amounts of Old Spice. That meant I was flooded with memories of the only other loser I had ever known who wore as much of that particular brand: Father Seamus.

Suddenly, instead of worrying about getting shot in the head, I had a whole different set of traumas to overcome. Traumas that had become old friends in the way FDR was old friends with Hitler.

I've tried to ignore these old pals over the years, and sometimes I actually think I have overcome them, but then they rear their ugly heads and Father Seamus is suddenly floating around in my psyche, making me wish I had a chance to put him into that *ultimate suffering machine* that William Goldman invented for *The Princess Bride*.

Because it wouldn't be enough to just kill the guy. I would have to make him suffer like that so you could hear his screams for miles and miles. I always believed I would have enjoyed that.

Then I became aware that Sasquatch was yelling at me about turning left. I actually felt relief when I got out of Father Seamus's room in my head and back into the life-threatening trip to visit with Uncle Max.

Pretty soon, we arrived at a seedy office building in Huntington Beach. Downtown Huntington played host to many dark streets, including this one, where a building that had seen better days seemed the perfect home for the business operations of Max Dimitrios, Esq.

Two large men bookended the front door. They were better dressed but considerably smaller than Sasquatch.

I named them *Ike and Mike*.

Ike reached out and opened my car door while Mike opened the rear door to the building. By this time I had stopped worrying and started looking for an opportunity. Worrying is destructive at times like that, so you need to concentrate only on your shot. Even if it's a million-to-one shot. That's your only hope, and you have to go for it, because gangster headquarters like these are like Roach Motels, you check in, but you don't check out.

It's sort of liberating to know you have almost no chance. Since you know you're as good as dead, you have an advantage over guys who think they might actually survive if they do what the bad guys tell them. I knew that these dudes were going to kill me no matter what, and that became my advantage because I had nothing to lose. But it's only a small advantage, because the statistics are always with the guys who carry the guns.

I felt ten percent better, but 23 percent less effective.

I noticed that Ike and Mike both wore shoulder holsters under their cheap suits. I noticed that we were going to the third floor in the elevator, and I noticed that all three guys, even Sasquatch, seemed a little nervous.

I thought I might be able to use their nervousness to my advantage. I lowered the odds against me to a thousand-to-one.

The odds changed back when we stepped out into the third floor hallway. Another behemoth stood outside the office door amid the crummy furniture and cases of Scotch. Not only that, I didn't know what to call this guy, because Ike and Mike only worked for two guys, so I decided to rename the former Ike as *Huey*, the former Mike as *Dewey*, and the new guy in the hall would be *Louie*.

Huey, Dewey, Louie and Sasquatch. Sounds like a bad sketch on Saturday Night Live, but at least I knew all the players I was up against.

The leg-breaker quartet ushered me past one of those old wooden doors that had a glass window inscribed with *Dimitrios Imports* in faded letters. The old man himself was sitting behind a huge desk in a worn swivel chair. He wore an expensive suit that didn't fit, a bad comb-over, and an expression of malice. His interlaced fingers were steepled as his hands rested on top of a large vest, which rested on top of a large stomach. His eyes were completely black, and he was the spitting image of that character actor who was in that Orson Welles movie where Charleton Heston played the police chief of Mexico.

"Akim Tamiroff?"

"YES! Akim Tamiroff."

And that wasn't all, he *sounded* like Akim Tamiroff. As soon as he opened his mouth, I forgot all about being scared and tried to remember who he looked like. I've never met a crook yet who wasn't stupid, and Uncle Max did nothing to change that opinion. He did what these guys always do in these situations. He tried to scare me. He narrowed his beady eyes and assumed a tough guy stance.

"I wanted to see what you looked like before I killed you."

Despite my situation, I almost laughed when I heard his cheesy accent. He waited for me to say something, but I was too busy looking for my opportunity, which made him angry.

"Hey I'm talkin' to you."

He motioned to Louie, who stepped in front of me and smiled. He probably expected me to cry, but I smiled right back because I knew something he didn't. I knew he was going to punch me, but I wasn't worried because most of these guys are lost when they fight someone who actually knows how to fight back.

Huey and Dewey each grabbed me by the arm so Louie would have a good shot at me. They all waited for me to say something, but I just kept smiling, which made them cock their heads at an angle like a dog when you ask him who pooped in the living room.

Louie telegraphed a roundhouse right, which is what I was hoping he would do. I tipped my head quickly and Louie's fist cracked against the top of my head, which is the hardest part of the body. I felt it, but Louie broke a couple of knuckles. He grabbed his fist in pain and hustled out of the room. Uncle Max was very unhappy and motioned to Dewey and Sasquatch, who grabbed me by the arms and nodded to Huey. Huey stepped in front of me and gave me a pretty good body punch to the stomach. I was able to cushion it slightly, but not much. I acted like it hurt more than it did to gain a little time. I moaned like a backyard cat and made them stop to determine if I was sincere or faking it. These morons should have kept hitting me, but when I started in with the wounded act, they just stood there watching me. They let go and I fell to my knees in front of the big desk.

Finally, they started moving back in. I leaned forward onto the big desk next to a large snow globe with all the snowflakes resting on the bottom. When I felt Huey reaching for me I recognized my opportunity.

I grabbed the snow globe off the desk and pounded Huey over the head with it, stunning him enough so I could grab his gun with my left hand. By this time, Sasquatch had his gun out, and in one motion, I pitched the snow globe like a fastball and pounded Sasquatch in the face. I heard his nose crunch as he dropped his gun arm and fell behind a big chair. I was over the desk like Spider Man and had Uncle Max in a headlock before Dewey could get his gun out. By the time he had the gun pointed it me, I was using Max as my bulletproof vest.

Huey was wandering around the room in a daze while I held his gun to his boss's head. Dewey and Sasquatch were pointing their guns at me, or rather, at Max, but I knew something they didn't.

"Okay fellas, let's all take a deep breath," said Max.

I shot Sasquatch through the comfy chair. I estimated that the shot hit him between his pectoral muscles. He reacted reflexively, he shot back, only he didn't hit me, he hit Max in the arm.

"Ow! Dammit, you idiot."

"I wouldn't be too tough on him Uncle Max. He's on your side."

"I mean, it's all right, Lyle."

Sasquatch had been shot directly in the heart and was bleeding profusely. In the movies, he would drop like a rock, but in real life, you can hang on for quite a while with a wound like he had However, he was fading fast and he lowered himself to the floor with a thud.

"My name is Steve," said Sasquatch.

"Really? You look like a Lyle," replied Uncle Max.

I noticed Dewey was getting into position on my right, so I waited until he had it, and yanked Uncle Max back into his direction. Dewey shot Max in his other arm.

"Ow! Come on! What's wrong with you idiots?"

"Nice shootin' fellas. I take it Uncle Max doesn't give you guys time off for target practice."

"Look, McCoy, I want to make a deal. I know you're not stupid. I can make you rich. I'm sure we can work something out. You can have anything you want."

"But I don't want anything I want as much as I want you to be dead."

"Don't be stupid. If you kill me, they kill you. You're not willing to die just to kill me."

"I wouldn't be so sure Uncle Max. They turned off my cable service last week."

Max reacted in confusion while Sasquatch slumped behind the cozy chair. He was bleeding out and losing consciousness. He raised his gun and waved it around, seemingly without direction. We all got caught up in watching the weapon wave hither and yon. I was checking on Dewey when Sasquatch finally pulled the trigger. The bullet started careening around the room like a pinball. It ricocheted off the iron radiator, then off an old television sitting in the corner. Finally, it caromed off a bronze bust of Aristotle before it hit Huey right through the heart.

Huey looked like he had won the lottery. He had a big smile on his face and his eyes were wide open. He stood motionless for a moment, then dropped onto his face like a tree felled by a lumberjack. Dewey, however, was untouched and planning his move. He tried to shoot again, but I yanked Max toward him just like the last time, and again, Max took one of Dewey's bullets in the shoulder.

"Ow! You Moron! Can't you do anything right?"

"Easy there chief. You're really burning your bridges. Now Dewey over there knows that his life isn't worth much after he shoots the boss TWICE. He's thinking to himself that the best thing for him to do would be to shoot us both."

"What?"

"He's right too. You wouldn't let him live after this."

"Sure I would."

"Do you believe him Dewey? Because I don't."

"My name's not Dewey, its Horace."

"Really?"

"Now HIS name I knew."

"How long have you been working for this scumbag?"

"You know, I have feelings," said Max.

"Oh shut up. The smart thing for Horace to do is to shoot us both, but his only chance would be to shoot right through you and take me out at the same time."

I could tell this planted a seed with Horace, who took his gun off of me and aimed it straight at Uncle Max's heart. That's what I was waiting for. The moment he lowered his gun, I shot him right through the forehead. He wavered in place for a minute, before spiraling into a heap on the floor.

Sasquatch and Huey were already dead, and Max was weak from loss of blood. I let him fall over onto his desk and pointed my gun at the door waiting for Louie to come back. Then I heard a car engine start outside. I looked through the window and saw Louie peel out, destination unknown.

I rolled Max over onto his back on the big desk and climbed on top of him.

"What in the hell was this all for?"

He was groggy, and probably couldn't even hear me, but I was ticked off.

"I paid you the money and a big bonus. Why did you keep coming after me?"

He couldn't answer me. He was fading fast. I slapped him a couple of times trying to bring him back, but he just kept drooling. And then the door busted open and you joined the party. The next thing I knew, the room was lousy with coppers.

"We got an anonymous tip."

"And this time you made sure the cuffs were a little bit tighter."

"Yeah, but you still got away. One of these days you're gonna have to show me how you do that."

"Maybe when you're old enough."

"Let me give you a little of the story from my vantage point."

"Please."

"I bust into a mobster's place of business, expecting it to be an ambush, and I find three dead guys on the floor, with you about to kill the big boss."

"I wasn't gonna kill him. I wanted to find out who…"

"Who what?"

"Who was really in charge."

"What makes you think he was working for somebody else?"

"If he had been in charge he would have had Sasquatch plug me with the two goons in the shower."

"Maybe he wanted to beat on you a little. You know, to make an example of you."

"Nah, he had something else in mind."

"Did you ever find out what it was?"

"Yes, but..."

"But what?"

"That part comes later."

CHAPTER ELEVEN
Anaheim Prison Blues

The next thing I knew, I was sitting across a familiar metal table. Detective Dick was facing me, sitting in an opposing chair without having removed his hands from his pockets. I had been arrested enough times to know that you always stow your cigarettes and lighter in your socks. Sometimes you get lucky and the cops don't check there. In this case, however, the cops had checked and confiscated my Lucky Strikes, but they hadn't checked the other sock closely enough to notice the roll of singed hundreds against my ankle.

Detective Dick sat motionless, refusing to blink or say anything. Although I was no stranger to the criminal justice system, I had nowhere near the experience that this guy had.

"So you're a writer."

I nodded.

"And have I read anything you wrote?"

"Hard to say."

"Try me."

"My first book was called, The Taste of Blood."

Jones just shook his head.

"Never heard of it Hemingway. Anything else?"

"I doubt it."

"Then maybe you can write something for me. Take that yellow pad and write down how you killed all those guys at the Dimitrios headquarters, and why you were trying to kill the big boss."

"First, I didn't kill all of them."

"Maybe some of them died of old age?"

"I'll tell you after my lawyer gets here."

"Really?"

"No, not really."

Jones straightened his tie and smoothed the front of his jacket. The expression in his eyes was a little scary, but I was confident he wasn't my biggest problem at that point. He suddenly stood up and barked at a uniform standing by the door.

"Open it!"

The uniform opened the door, Jones stomped through it, and I turned to the uniform unlocking my handcuffs from the metal chair with a paper clip I liberated from a desk on the way in.

"Got a cigarette?"

"Up yours, convict."

I had never been to the Anaheim Jail before, but one jailhouse looks pretty much like another from the inside. I was somehow comforted by the fact that this station was right next to the main library. Don't ask me why. However, since I had no escape route I had to lock the cuffs again.

Processing was tedious and uncomfortable as it always is, but for some reason the coppers were in a rush to get me before a judge. As a result, I also had to drop my paper clip before they searched me. I hadn't eaten anything since the Crab Cooker shrimp and I was starving. In fact, I was so hungry that I was even looking forward to the jailhouse chow. I sat in my cell next to a smelly loser named Simon who had been booked on a drunk and disorderly. I was happy when they opened the cell because it probably meant we were going to eat. However, I quickly found out we weren't getting chow, but an escort to court. I would now spend the next several hours strapped to Smelly Simon.

Anaheim doesn't have a court system, so they drove us to the Santa Ana courthouse in one of those large ugly vans where the windows are so dirty you can't even see out of them. The ride took about twenty minutes, but I doubled that time due to the smelly factor. There were ten of us altogether, handcuffed into five pairs. Finally, they opened the van doors and ushered us down a concrete hallway into the bowels of the civic center.

We stood in that hall, without moving for about thirty minutes. This isn't unusual. The wheels of justice grind slowly. The concrete hallway was as filthy as the prisoners, and I guess I'm getting soft, because I just couldn't get used to the nastiness of it all.

Finally, they ordered us to sit on the floor against the wall. Each of the five pairs sat casually with a modicum of grumbling. Then I noticed something that could make a difference: a large wooden kitchen match that was on the floor, within reach. Smelly Simon was so out of it he didn't even notice when I picked it up, but I didn't intend to use it unless another opportunity arose. It would do me no good to free myself from the handcuffs only to add a charge of attempting to escape from custody.

So I palmed the match and held onto it; just in case. Then the guards told us all to stand, which we did, and to walk forward on their command. We started walking and continued for about thirty steps, into the next section of hallway. Then after another thirty-minute rest stop, the guards again told us to sit down against the wall.

Some of the prisoners chatted about their women, their cars, or their ordeals with the criminal justice system. I watched the guards duck out of the hallway as soon as we sat down. Apparently they didn't like the smell any better than I did, and they were seeking some relief. I made a note of that door as a potential exit route, but the guards were standing in the way.

Finally, we were ushered into the defendant section of Courtroom B. We sat on benches that reminded me of the choir pews in the Orphanage Chapel where I grew up, except these pews were located behind iron mesh that separated the lawbreakers from the citizens. We were each handcuffed to the pew, but I managed to keep my kitchen match hidden.

The guards told us that Judge James Pierce would be presiding and that he was tough, but fair. This made me think about my life and what I had done with it.

I wondered if what I had done to Phoebe was fair.

I wondered if I would ever see her again.

I wondered what had happened to me. How had I changed so much over a couple of crummy days? Would my life ever return to normal? Did I even want to go back to normal?

For a guy who doesn't like to examine his feelings too closely, I was diving pretty deep.

Then, I got a break from my introspection when the lights went out.

As you might imagine, this is pretty unusual for that type of venue. There are no windows in the Santa Ana courtrooms, so everyone sat in complete, soupy blackness. The guards were all shouting for everyone to keep calm, and lawyers in attendance were all asking each other for tips on finding an exit. Most of the prisoners sat still, but I took advantage of the opportunity to unlock my handcuffs using the kitchen match. I didn't move, in case the lights came back on and I had to click the cuffs back into place.

But a funny thing was happening to me. I had a feeling that this darkness was for my benefit, and that something was going to happen that would be advantageous.

Don't ask me why. I've never been the type of guy who got feelings.

Then something happened.

I heard Phoebe whisper, "this way."

I was surprised I recognized her whisper and more surprised she was breaking me out. Then I realized I should never be surprised by anything she does.

I slipped out of my cuffs and traveled in the direction of Phoebe's voice. Then I noticed a sliver of light in front of me, like a doorway into a hall. When the door opened, I could see the light spill onto Phoebe's beautiful face, Rembrandt-style, and I was so excited I grabbed her and kissed her, like I wasn't a convict in the middle of a breakout. Go figure.

"You can't do this. Get out of here."

"Shut up and follow me. I've got this caper all figured."

"Caper?"

"Move it!"

She pulled me through the door. For the first time in my life I was worried what would happen to the girl. I knew this would be very bad for her if we got caught, but I also knew that if I didn't go with her she would almost certainly get caught by herself. I followed her, but the guards noticed and gave chase.

It seemed like we had 35 guards on our collective tail. We ran about 50 feet to the end of the hall where a window was open. Phoebe didn't say anything; she just lifted her leg over the windowsill and jumped out, so I did the same without thinking about our location on the third floor. The next thing I knew, I was airborne, dropping like a rock toward the back of a pickup truck with a bunch of sofa cushions in the bed.

Phoebe hit the cushions and bounced forward. I hit the cushions right after her and bounced over the side of the truck onto the ground. The pickup immediately pulled away just before a guard who must have followed us out the window hit the ground with a crunch. I wasn't hurt because my fall had been broken by the cushions, but the guard was wiggling on the ground grabbing his feet in pain. He looked like he would live, and he was so involved in his injury he never drew his weapon, so I got up and caught the pickup, jumping into the bed just before we pulled around the corner and out of sight.

The guy driving the truck looked Mexican, and I wondered if he might be a relative of Phoebe's.

"Who's the driver?"

"I don't know his name. I hired him and his truck at Home Depot for fifty bucks."

"Great. Tell him to pull over."

She spoke to him in Spanish. I was impressed by her fluency, and when I say, impressed, I mean, turned on. It seemed that there was no limit to Phoebe's ability to get me hot. The Mexican pulled over and I dragged Phoebe out of the truck. I waved to him and he drove off smiling, seemingly unconcerned that he had just committed a felony, then I hailed a cab and opened the door for Phoebe to get in. She jumped a little when I shut the door behind her.

"What are you doing?"

I handed the driver a hundred bucks.

"Don't stop until you get to Fullerton."

He was ready to hit the gas all the way to Oregon, but Phoebe didn't like watching from the sidelines.

"No way. I'm coming with you."

I stepped back and looked her right in the eyes.

"Look Baby, what I have to do you can't be any part of."

"That's from a movie."

"But it's true. Go home and stay there."

I motioned with my thumb for the driver to hit the gas.

"Vamanos!"

He did, and I watched as Phoebe disappeared into the sunset.

CHAPTER TWELVE
Call me Jack

While the sirens wailed all around me, I walked as deliberately as I could to another cab sitting around the corner. I told the driver to head for Newport, figuring the cops wouldn't look for me in the same place where the previous night's bloodbath had occurred. I checked into a different fleabag hotel and walked over to the Crab Cooker for another order of the shrimp with starchy potatoes. I had been craving it ever since people started shooting at me. You must try this joint when you are in Newport, and don't forget to start with the clam chowder.

After dinner, I walked back to the proverbial scene of the crime. It looked like you might imagine, with crime scene tape and chalk marks on the ground. I wandered cautiously to the trash area around back and emptied the trashcan I had used to hide Leo's guns. After all of the cornflakes and beer cans emptied onto the ground I spotted the new Colt 45 and brushed off the residue. Then I tossed the garbage back on top of the remaining guns and hoofed it back to my new room.

By this time, I had become accustomed to hoodlums and other creatures lying in wait, so when I approached the door, I had cocked the Colt I was holding in my right hand and approached the door as I had been taught in the Army. Most guys lost fights because they were unwilling to go all the way, but both the Army and boxing taught me that I had to be prepared to destroy my opponent in order to survive, so I was ready to do whatever it took if somebody jumped me.

I'm not a big gun guy, but I never like to attempt a job unless I have the right tools. I thought I heard a slight noise in the hotel room; so I slammed the door all the way open in case somebody was behind it. I probably used a bit too much caution because I busted a round hole in the wall where the doorknob slammed into it, but no one was actually in the room, so I locked the door behind me and searched every inch of the place.

After being especially cautious checking the bathroom and closet I went back into the bathroom to double-check and noticed an absence of noise for the first time in recent memory. It sounded sweet. I just stood there, letting the quiet pour over me and enjoying the absence of craziness. Then I thought I heard something in the room I had just searched. I made sure the safety was off, then let the Colt lead me carefully back into the room.

I was covered, but I wasn't prepared for what I saw.

John Fitzgerald Kennedy; 35th President of the United States was relaxing in one of two ugly chairs next to an ugly table. I probably had him covered, but after a series of supernatural experiences I still wasn't ready for the sight of this guy.

He was strikingly handsome with what they used to call a Pepsodent smile. His legs were crossed and his hands were stretched out on the arms of the chair. He didn't seem the slightest bit worried that I had a gun pointed at him. Instead of the dark suits he wore during the debates, he sported a tweed sports coat over a dress shirt, and his open collar featured a silk ascot. The overall result was movie star meets college professor. This guy had real star quality.

His face was recognizable the world over, but somehow he looked different than the pictures I had seen. He was tanned and relaxed as always, but he seemed to have gained a few pounds and the extra weight added to his vitality. His hair was tousled and gray around the edges.

While smiling at me, he removed an impressive-looking cigar from his inside pocket. Then he spent some time lighting it with a gleaming platinum Zippo. Then he smiled again and motioned for me to sit in the other chair.

"You would think I would hate all products associated with Cuba, but there is nothing like a Cuban cigar. Fortunately these are pre-embargo."

He offered one to me, and I took it, but slid it into my jacket pocket for later, just in case it might have been a trap.

"I take it you know who I am."

I nodded, or at least I think I nodded.

"You don't need the heater, Soldier, I'm here to help."

I wasn't prepared for the colloquial vernacular, but I kept my guard up.

"Let's just say we'll keep Mr. Colt around for sentimental reasons."

"Suit yourself. But you've got a problem, Soldier, and we don't have much time."

"Excuse me Mr. President, but how do I know I can trust you?"

"You know, that's a good point. All I can tell you is that the-uh front office has taken an interest in your case and they sent me to help. You must know all about me. Does that help you determine which side I am on?"

"Frankly, no Mr. President, after everything I have heard about your private life."

"Good point, Soldier, and I suppose I deserve your ah-scrutiny. Would it make you feel any better if I told you that even though I was a sinner in my life--in fact I was a world-class sinner, but that I was saved by grace?"

"Really? I would have thought all of your sins would have been tough to overcome."

"They were; they required one very large sacrifice."

"Okay, I'm not convinced, but I will listen to your offer."

"Well, the first thing we have to do is to get you out of here, because the coppers are on the way."

"Coppers?"

"I know, it's cheesy, but I was never allowed certain American idioms while I was alive, and I find it amusing to indulge in them now that I no longer have to maintain a public ah-profile."

Even though this guy was an American hero *and* American history, my lifetime of experience told me not to trust him. Most of the people I had trusted in my life had betrayed me with abandon. But how can you not trust President Kennedy? I had to make a choice, so I shoved the Colt into my belt and held the door open for him.

"After you Mr. President."

He got up, adjusted his cuffs like Cary Grant, picked up his Cuban and pointed his index finger at me like a pistol.

"Call me Jack."

He glided past me and into the parking lot. The president had taken possession of a brand new, gleaming black Crown Vic. Apparently heaven must have some sort of a fleet deal with Ford. Jack jumped into the passenger seat and motioned for me to drive. I eased out of the parking lot just before several police cars blazed into the lot and established a perimeter. I was once again learning the rules after the game had already started, so I tried to pump the president for information.

"So where are you from?"

"Harvard College; class of 1940."

"No, I mean, where in the spiritual realm?"

"Oh, well, I'm not sure you could really understand the directions, but you can safely assume that I am not from the same place as those losers with whom you've been ah-dealing."

"So, you're from heaven?"

133

"Yes, that's right."

"Then you're an angel?"

"I'm a fixer. In every election or every contest in life you must have someone who knows which palms to grease and which heads to chop. They don't really have a name for my job, which is one of the reasons I like doing it. And we're not so hung up on the semantics of corporate structure in heaven. Just know that the chief executive is letting me help out with a few cases before I retire."

"A fixer?"

"Think Bob Haldeman, think Chuck Colson, think Ted Sorensen."

I had no idea who any of those guys were, but I thought it was best to just nod as though I did. Meeting the president further disturbed my understanding of the relationship between good and evil. Why would God send a guardian angel or fixer if I had already signed away my soul? Why hadn't I heard from J. Parnell? And how can a world-class womanizer like Jack Kennedy still be forgiven and go to heaven? As we cruised down Pacific Coast Highway, my new pal Jack gazed out the window, watching the coastline go by.

"This reminds me of Hyannis Port. I could have easily lived my entire life as a beach bum. There's something so peaceful about the beach; it's as though you're caught up in the warm embrace of the almighty.

Once you have the coastline in your blood you never really get over it; do you? After I was shot in Dallas, I had a lot of stuff going on inside my head. Even if you die right away the process is lengthy and you really do have a lot to think about. Anyway, while I lay dying my thoughts came back to the beach. I remembered a day when I was a kid. It had been a completely ordinary summer day in every way. We played football in the morning, we read Mark Twain in the afternoon, and we cooked hot dogs over an open fire after the sun went down. Isn't that odd? All of the places I eventually went and all of the things that happened in my life, and my final thoughts on earth were about a weenie roast."

I didn't know what to say, except that it was sort of odd.

"So now my job is to stop you from making the deal with Thomas. I worked with that guy, and I know what I'm talking about."

"It's too late. I already signed; in blood."

Jack took another long look at the coastline, and then re-lit his Cuban. He placed it in his mouth for a moment and blew out a long, perfect stream of smoke.

"Let's take a little drive."

I shrugged and merged into the fast lane heading south toward Laguna. Everything was beautiful for a moment. The sky was golden, the sea was blue and the air was clear. I could almost smell the Coppertone.

Then I heard a thunderclap and suddenly I was driving though a black tunnel with no light whatsoever.

The only things I could see were illuminated by my headlights. As far as I could tell, the ground, the walls and maybe even the ceiling above us were all dirt. It was like I was driving through a giant gopher hole. Dirt was flying in every direction, creating a dust storm that reduced visibility to virtually nothing. Rocks and pebbles bounced off the windshield and the shock absorbers seemed to be withstanding considerably more than the maximum amount of shock. This was a little too rough even for a Crown Vic, so I took my foot off the gas.

"I-ah wouldn't do that Soldier. Look what's behind us."

I glanced in the rear view mirror half ex-pecting to see the Taliban, but instead, I saw a wall of flames shooting through the tunnel toward us. It felt like I was in a Nicholas Cage movie, so I hit the gas and just barely avoided getting roasted.

"Hey, good for you."

"How do I get out of here?"

"Practice, practice, practice."

I was in a life-threatening situation and the dead president in my passenger seat was making jokes. That is a sentence I hope to never say again. The Crown Vic was doing 80 miles an hour, the engine was screaming and the flames were licking at the brand new paint on the trunk where the gas tank was located. If that wasn't enough, the road ahead was filled with all kinds of debris, like washing machine parts, basketball hoops, dead bodies and big cages like the ones used to keep sharks from eating the divers. I had to weave in and out of the debris to avoid crashing or ripping off the Crown Vic's undercarriage. The speedometer passed 90, but I couldn't pull away from the flames. For his part, Jack sat there watching the scene with the same emotion as a Driver's Ed teacher. I was freaking out and hot, but he seemed perfectly cool, puffing occasionally on the Cuban.

"You are a pretty good driver, Soldier."

I was about to say thank you when I noticed something bad--real bad.

On the horizon was a cliff, and I was heading directly toward it. I could tell it was a cliff because a glowing red light was bursting from what I assumed was the canyon on the other side. It basically looked like a nuclear bomb had exploded and we were hurtling toward the resulting radiation. I was caught between a wall of flame and a nuclear reaction, which, as you might imagine, was a first for me.

"Any suggestions?"

"Yeah, thanks for asking. Right after you pass that old vending machine, slam on your emergency brake and crank the wheel to the right as far as it will go. If you hit it just right, we'll make it onto that side road along the cliff."

"And what happens if I don't hit it just right?"

"Well, then we plunge into the eternal lake of fire."

"And that would be bad."

"You'll find out if the deal with Thomas goes through."

By this time, the flames were all over the back end of the Crown Vic. I could smell the paint and the plastic bumper melting. My head was filled with thoughts of more car explosions than a Jerry Bruckheimer movie. Meanwhile, Jack just sat there, puffing on his Cuban like he was enjoying the ride. It was hard to tell over the deafening noises all around me, but I think I actually heard him whistle. We were coming up on the point of no return when Jack leaned toward me.

"Okay Soldier, here it comes."

The Crown Vic was covered in flames, hurtling toward the abyss, and the speedometer read 100.

"Now!"

I slammed on the emergency brake. The car banked hard to the right, and skidded sideways past the pile of debris. It felt like we had more than enough momentum to carry us over the cliff, and I was completely helpless in the slide as I watched the scenery pass north to south across my front windshield. Jack leaned toward me like the PT Boat Captain he had been and calmly issued his commands.

"Stand by full throttle."

My foot hovered over the gas pedal like a helicopter, but I resisted the urge to go early.

"All ahead full, Soldier. Go! Go! Go!"

I shoved my foot down on the throttle and got the rear wheels to grab just in time to speed off on the cliffside road. I was afraid the flames would follow us, but I looked in the rear view mirror and saw the long tube of flames fly over the cliff in one long motion, like Lemmings, doomed to destruction. Jack just smiled at me like he knew exactly how it was going to turn out.

"Good job. All the chief asks is that we follow instructions The Army trained you well."

I slammed on the brakes and the car swerved to a stop. I turned to the president to find out what was next, but before I could say a word, the Crown Vic was suddenly swarmed by the same type of stupid-looking Blinkers that had attacked Phoebe in the Hummer; only these dudes were not playing possum. They were all claws and fangs, and they wanted in.

"Better keep moving Soldier. This is a bad neighborhood."

These Blinkers were nasty, and this time they looked more like John C. Reilly than Edward G. Robinson. I noticed they also had scars, but their scars were only on one side of their faces, almost like question marks. It looked like each separate gang in this neighborhood had different identifying scars. I hit the gas and watched in the mirror as the Blinkers tumbled off the car.

"When can I stop?"

"Never kid. That's the whole point. It's why your pal Parnell looks the way he does."

"But you look great."

"That's because I don't live here. I'm just a tour guide."

"What kind of tour?"

"I brought you here to show you one thing—

the other side of that cliff we just missed. That big glow is the payoff for everyone who makes a deal like the one you just signed."

I had resisted looking at it for fear of what was actually over there, but I managed to look and saw a glowing pit; a lake of fire. I could hear noises that sounded like wailing; crying like wounded animals moaning for their lives, or like parents grieving over dying children, or like lovers separated from their hearts. It sounded like all of those noises at once, multiplied by a hundred. These souls in the lake were doomed, like they were burning alive, but never burned completely. It was as though the agony somehow never ended.

"That's what your pal Parnell has to offer you. He's got to bring a soul back to hell with him. That's why he got a pass. If he doesn't bring back *your* soul, it gets worse for him down here."

"How could it possibly get worse?"

"You would be surprised, Soldier. You would be surprised."

"But I already made the deal."

"Okay, then here's what I recommend…"

Suddenly, a brick flew through the passenger side window knocking the president's Cuban from his grasp. When we looked up, hundreds of Blinkers dressed like storm troopers were running toward the car and Jack stopped in mid comment.

"Oh damn."

He jumped out of the car, slammed the door behind him and shouted at me through the hole in the window.

"Drive straight ahead and don't turn off this road for any reason! Don't take your foot off the gas until you reach the end of the road!"

I couldn't believe he was climbing out among all those miserable, nasty beasts.

"You can't go out there with those monsters."

"Don't worry about me Soldier; I was in Congress for 14 years. Now punch it, AND DON'T LOOK BACK!"

Jack ran about twenty feet from the car and started fighting like Jackie Chan. There was no evidence whatsoever of his fabled bad back or other health problems. Blinkers were flying through the air like cartoon characters, and exploding all over the president's silk ascot. I was captivated by the sight of Jack Kennedy fighting off evil like his old literary idol James Bond. Then, I noticed a few of the little mongrels as they started running toward me, so I did like my fixer said and hit the gas.

One of the Blinkers ran into my path with what looked like a bazooka. He assumed a combat stance, pointed it at me and fired. My time in the Army taught me that a bazooka shell through the face would be bad, so I leaned over onto the bench seat just in time to feel the shell explode through the windshield, over my head, and through the back window. Then I looked up just in time to see the offending Blinker holding his empty bazooka. The Crown Vic plowed into him and he was slammed fifty feet into the air in front of me. I could hear his munchkin squeal as he flew straight as an arrow and landed in my path. I thought about swerving to avoid him, but before I could decide, I felt the thump-thump of the car running over him like a speed bump. The resulting explosion sprayed purple goo onto my back window.

I kept driving faster and faster, the Crown Vic bounced and shook, but didn't break. Thank God for Dearborn engineering. I was soon plowing forward at 110 miles per hour. I finally came upon what looked like a border inspection station, and a huge neon sign blinked, *Prepare to stop*. Blinkers in uniforms ran out in front of the black and yellow striped arm and waved their hands for me to stop. I took Jack's advice and ignored the command, bashing through the Blinkers and the barrier. After clearing the station, I was immediately confronted with a three-way fork in the road. I stayed on the middle road and soon had three huge vehicles on my tail that looked like they were straight out of *Mad Max*.

These were tanks that had been put together with war surplus parts. All of them were equipped with big guns mounted on their roofs and manned by Blinkers with ugly scars and nasty dispositions. The guns were firing automatic rounds and I was beginning to wonder why I hadn't been hit when I realized these tanks were bouncing even worse than I was. The Blinkers couldn't aim because they were hanging on for dear life, or whatever they called it. The shells were exploding all around me. The dashboard, the windshield and the passenger seat all suffered tremendous damage, but I hadn't been hit yet.

The tanks were also fast, however, and I couldn't outrun them. Fortunately, the road was straight, because we were in total blackness, lit only by my remaining headlights and the weak light provided by the surplus lamps on the tanks.

My speedometer was pinned at 120, and the tanks were still gaining on me and still shooting. Then the two outside tanks pulled up on either side of me and the one behind me finally managed to score a hit, taking off most of my passenger side roof. Suddenly, I was driving a low-rent convertible.

As the two outside tanks came alongside me, they both turned their cannons toward me. I went against Jack's warning and slammed on the brakes. The side cannons both locked on me and the tank that was following me slammed into what was left of my trunk, deploying my air bags. I couldn't see what happened, but from the sound, I could tell that the side tanks had both fired at once, hitting each other because I was no longer in the middle. I yanked the air bag down and hit the gas, flying through shrapnel and debris. Fortunately, my engine didn't stall and I took off. When I checked the mirror, I could see the rear tank lose control as it got smaller in my view. It rolled and exploded in a glow so bright I was temporarily blinded by the flash off of my rearview mirror.

I couldn't see anything except my headlights on the ground in front of me. The road got even nastier and I could hear the Crown Vic straining against the stress. Even New York cabs don't have to put up with this much abuse. I thought about changing direction to see if I could find a way out, but decided to listen to the guy with the Harvard degree. I was going to keep going straight as long as the car kept running.

I was in the darkness for a few moments longer.

Then the bumps disappeared and the road smoothed out. I could see by my headlights that I was on smooth blacktop. It was quiet.

Too quiet.

I got the feeling that I was nearing the end of an arduous journey; one which I might not survive. But I had a feeling like the one you get when you are dancing and the song is about to end.

Then the music stopped.

I crashed through a barrier and was blinded by light.

Then I was airborne.

I had broken through a brittle barrier and was flying over rush hour traffic passing South Coast Plaza. That's right; I was flying *over* the traffic. The scene seemed to be happening in slow motion and all I could do was hang onto the steering wheel and hope for the best. I guess I was shooting out of another dimension or something. Then the motion seemed to get faster; much faster. I slammed four wheels down onto concrete with extreme prejudice.

Since I had no air bags left, my face broke my fall against the steering wheel. I saw stars and felt pain; lots of it. But I had emerged from the Lake of Fire alive, and that seemed very special to me.

I recognized my location, sliding through the intersection of Warner and Bristol. The car hopped over a curb and landed perfectly situated in a Carl's Jr. drive through lane. Since I had no alternative, I ordered a Coke. I wanted to stop, but I didn't dare. The Crown Vic had a roasted paint job, the roof was peeled back like the lid of a tuna can, and there was busted glass fore and aft. The gal at the Carl's window seemed concerned about the steam rising from the car but gently handed me the soda. I pulled into traffic as inconspicuously as possible and tried to blend in with the other cars.

I kept moving until I got onto the Newport Freeway and headed back toward Yorba Linda.

CHAPTER THIRTEEN
I'm Talking To You

After racing through the nether region, the Newport Freeway seemed 29 percent easier to navigate, but I was in a hurry to see Phoebe's face again. Something about her was under my skin and I needed to scratch.

I also needed to pee.

I had to see her again.

"I knew that."

"Yeah, well, this was all new to me, and I was pretty darn unsure of myself."

"So how were you going to find her?"

"I knew I couldn't find her, but that she would find me."

"How could she do that?"

"The same way she did before, she would draw on her mysterious, freaky supernatural powers."

The sun was setting to my left, and if I hadn't been so completely frustrated by my situation I probably would have enjoyed the view. I left the freeway at Imperial and cruised through Yorba Linda. I circled the Nix a few times before parking on the street. Everything was closed and no one was around, so I used the bushes as camouflage while I relieved my aching bladder. I thought I was safe, but immediately after committing myself I sensed her presence.

"That's gross."

"Was it her?"

"No."

"Really?"

"No, not really. Of course it was her."

I couldn't stop, so I finished what I was doing and looked up. The sky caught my attention once again. This time I noticed it was deep blue, illuminated by the lights of Orange County and blanketed by a sea of puffy white clouds. It looked too good to be real. I wondered if Phoebe had brought it with her.

"I knew you would find me."

"I knew that you knew I would."

"What is this, a Jackie Gleason routine?"

"Who's Jackie Gleason?"

"Never mind. Are you okay?"

"I'm fine. What happened to you?"

"Let me ask you the same question."

"Are you referring to what happened over there on the street?

"No, I'm referring to when the car drove RIGHT THROUGH YOU on the street."

She smiled and took my arm like she was walking me down the aisle.

"I need you to go someplace with me."

She took one look at the Crown Vic and turned to me with a smile.

"I hope your insurance is paid up."

She motioned for me to climb into the passenger seat of her car, a cherry red Karman Ghia. She let the engine warm up for a nanosecond, then punched it and roared off into the wiles of Yorba Linda. She drove like she did everything else: full tilt. I was soon wondering if this ride might be more dangerous than the one I took with JFK.

After passing a sign that said, "Welcome to Anaheim," we pulled into the parking lot of *The Rock*. The sign in front said it was a Foursquare Church, which was all the information I needed to tell me I was in the wrong place. I could hear the rollicking gospel music coming from the auditorium and it made me very nervous. Catholics were one thing, but Evangelicals were something else, man.

"I hope you don't expect me to go in there with you, because I am no Christian, Honey."

She once again did that thing with her face where she reduced me to rubble while barely changing expressions. I decided to resist the urge to poke the bear further.

"No one's asking you to speak in tongues. Just come in and listen for a minute. You might even learn something about your predicament."

"What predicament is that?"

"How should I know? You're the one who's getting his car all blown up by demons."

I could have said no to her, but somehow I didn't want to say no to her. That was weird. Then I realized I hadn't told Phoebe about the ride with JFK *or* the demons. It meant that she might just have known something I didn't, so I decided to find out just what was the source of her power; even if it meant darkening the doors of *The Rock*.

We got out of the car and started walking toward the church, from whence the muffled music came. There were several people at the front doors wearing smiles I didn't believe. I've seen this type of thing before, and I was convinced these two *greeters* were brainwashed, Kool-Aid drinking acolytes who had no will of their own and practiced smiling using 10 percent more teeth than necessary. The minions opened the doors wide and we passed through. Knowing my record with the church, I half expected those doors to blow off the building as I did.

The blaring music was not like anything I had ever heard growing up at the Catholic orphanage. It was more like a rock concert than a mass. A big guy with a fashionably shaved head stood at the front of the stage playing keyboards while leading the congregation and choir. He wore a black suit with an open-collared white shirt and pounded the keyboard while singing. He sounded like the guy from the Doobie Brothers.

The words to the songs were projected on huge screens overhead; the choir and other backup singers clapped and swayed to the music while the big guy controlled the moment. Rather than sitting like civilized parishioners, the members of the audience were also on their feet clapping, swaying, raising their arms to the heavens, and seemingly blissed out on the experience of worshipping the Lord. The total effect was a lot to take.

I didn't get it, but the music and the atmosphere were infectious. I decided to steel myself against any possible influence. Phoebe led me toward a vacant seat in the back, but this music seemed to have all the reverence I remembered from the Catholic hymns combined with the beat of a Motown song.

I was nervous, not because I didn't like it, but because I did.

We eased into the standing room above our seats and stood clapping with all the other supplicants. Actually, Phoebe clapped while I stood with my hands in my pockets looking uncomfortable. She knew all the words and fell into the experience like she had been doing it all her life. I thought about singing, but then decided against it. I planned to just wait it out, find out what she wanted me to hear, and never come back here again.

Then the big guy in front looked up from his keyboard and did a double take when he saw me. This made me shudder. It looked like I was someone he had identified from *America's Most Wanted*. I don't know how he could even spot me in the crowd, but he made me. He made eye contact and kept it; like I owed him money.

I knew he was staring at me and he didn't make any attempt to hide it. He stopped playing and stood there with me in his sights. The band continued, the choir continued, and the blissed-out audience continued with the song, but the big guy and I were in a world of our own. He started pacing back and forth on the stage, but he never took his eyes off me. Then, he turned his back on the audience, raised his hands to the heavens and seemed to be saying something. The sisters never did anything even remotely like this. I wondered what was up with this freak.

"Why wasn't the choir stopping?" I asked myself. "Didn't they know the song leader was in another world?" But no one even seemed to notice. They just kept singing and waving their hands, like they didn't even need the big guy leading the songs. Even Phoebe didn't notice. She seemed totally into charismatic mode by this point, and uninterested in my little showdown with the big guy. There was no end in sight for the song.

Then the big guy ended it.

He walked to the center of the stage; held him arms out wide, and everyone stopped, fast. It was like a hose after the water has been abruptly turned off. The big guy did his thing and the room was suddenly silent. He stood there for a minute, then looked straight at me, pointed a meaty finger in my direction and shouted, "The word says, 'Come to me, all ye who labor and are heavy-laden, and I will give you rest'."

The big guy's intense, booming voice was still bouncing around the room when everyone suddenly turned in my direction. They all gave me a weird look, like they all knew something I didn't.

I looked at Phoebe for direction, but she was just smiling at me. The big guy was still pointing at me, and again, he made with the, "Come to me, all

ye who labor and are heavy-laden, and I will give
you rest" routine.

I have found that any time emotions enter
the picture it is a good time to leave, so I decided to
bolt. I shoved my way back through the blissed out
members of the congregation and slammed through
the swinging doors through which I had entered.
The two acolytes smiled even bigger as I exited.

"Thanks for coming!"

"See you next time."

I didn't look back to see if Phoebe was
coming after me. I only knew I wasn't prepared for
this crap.

What was going on? Did phoebe set this
whole thing up? How could she? I had never told
her about Patches and me, but maybe he told her
himself after he parted the traffic on Imperial. Then
I wondered if Patches was also there at The Rock.
I was suffocating in a spiritual video game and I
needed some air, lots of air.

I bobbed and weaved through the parking
lot heading toward my car. I took some comfort
from a little shadow boxing to ease the tension,
but then I remembered I had come with Phoebe.
Okay, so I would try for her car, but no sooner had I
spotted it, than I felt everything get squishy. I could
still see her car, but it seemed to be getting fuzzy.
Then I realized I was in trouble. Since I didn't see
it coming, I figured I had been smacked in the back
of the head with something heavy. Then, I realized
I was still getting pummeled from all sides.

A fist pounded me in the face, a boot landed in my side, and I was aware of hitting the ground, although I could barely feel anything. All I could hear was my own heartbeat. Everything else was low in the background. I was faintly aware of voices yelling, and I noticed the characters that were mugging me. Two of them were wearing the moronic tracksuits and sideways baseball caps that Leo's boys had displayed. The third was wearing an extra-shiny gold Italian suit, with gold cufflinks so big I could see them, even in my blurry state, and for the crowning triumph, he wore golden Mickey Mouse ears. I swear, the ears you get at Disneyland, and they were gold. By this time, I was too far gone to do anything about the dudes who were beating the crap out of me. I tried to react, but mostly I was just lying there taking a beating.

After a while, the hooligans seemed to get tired. I started to breathe again. I was able to focus a little better. I noticed the Mickey ears had something embroidered on them. It looked like it said, *Jimmy*, no, *Timmy*. This was a creepy sight to see just before passing out.

Timmy's golden ears slowly faded to black.

CHAPTER FOURTEEN
I Thought You Were Taller

When the lights came back on, I was folded up like an accordion in a luggage compartment behind the rear seat of a van. I bounced uncomfortably every time the van did, and that compounded the pain I was feeling from the beating. I'm no stranger to pain, and judging from the way I felt, this was among the worst beatings I had ever suffered. I wanted desperately to return to sleep, but if I hoped to survive this ride, I knew the first step was staying awake.

A handsome, powerfully built man with flowing bright red hair and freckles leaned over the rear seat and smiled at me. With his big hair and toothy smile, he reminded me of a cross between Eric Stoltz and Daniel Craig.

I was more than a little curious about who this guy was and why he was driving me to my doom, but I was a little too tired to do much about it.

When my eyes could focus a little better, I got a better look at the gold Mickey Mouse ears he was wearing. They had a patch that read, *Disneyland 50th Anniversary*. Then I had an ominous recollection. I had heard tales of a mob hit man named Timmy. I had even considered writing about him. Timmy was famous for his gold wardrobe and his brutality. I knew I was in his company, which wasn't good.

Then I noticed his scar.

He had a crescent-shaped line on his left cheek, from the corner of his mouth to just under his left ear. In Vegas, the tough guys at the orphanage used to call that, *the mark of the squealer*. I had heard guys threaten to inflict it, but I had never actually seen one. This was different from the scars I had seen on the Squealers, except that it was a scar on the face.

In spite of the scar, he was a very handsome guy with big shiny teeth.

He was pointing his evil grin and a big nasty gun in my direction. He must have been about thirty, with piercing blue eyes, and he had the whitest skin I had ever seen. His wardrobe was so shiny it illuminated the darkness surrounding us. Like a young David Bowie, he had a mysterious, almost feminine quality. Unlike Bowie, he had a lot to say.

"Rise and shine, Mister Sleepy. Did you have a nice nap?"

"I thought you were taller."

"You know who I am?"

"Aren't you Timmy, the big time hitter from L.A.?"

He looked impressed, then turned to his associates to see if they took note of his celebrity status.

"You heard of me, huh?"

"Oh yeah, except I never heard you were so obtuse."

His expression changed. He looked confused.

"I'm not obtuse. I only have 3 percent body fat."

That's not what it means.

He searched for a clever comeback.

"Really? Well I don't have to know what it means. Wanna know why?"

I didn't respond.

"Because I'm still gonna be alive in fifteen minutes, THAT'S WHY!" You're gonna be laying in a ditch, and you know what you're gonna be then?"

"Dead?"

"That's right."

Then we had an uncomfortable silence.

"Dead!"

"Right, dead, I get it."

Frankly, I was giving out with a lot more trash talk than I would have imagined in such a perilous situation. It was surprising, but I was just too tired to put up with any more crap.

Timmy was one of those people who, for whatever reason, looks smarter than he is. If you dressed him right, he could pass as a college professor or a diplomat, at least until he opened his mouth. I had heard that he worked for Dimitrios, but the news of his low conversational skills had somehow eluded me. Probably because most people he spoke with wound up dead.

"Why didn't Uncle Max cancel the contract?"

"He did, but someone else made up a new one."

"You mean that someone besides Dimitrios wants me dead?"

"That's right loser, and I'm gonna collect a bundle for your carcass."

I considered asking about the ears, but I was pretty sure I wouldn't like the answer.

My hands were tied with rope behind my back and my ankles were bound together with duct tape. I was shoved into the cargo area behind the rear seat, and although I couldn't see it in the darkened van, I assumed I was covered in blood. My lips felt swollen and my eyes were crusty and hard to open. Everything hurt, but the most painful thing was my wrists, because I was trying to wiggle out of the ropes that held them together.

People always think that there's some big trick that escape artists know. The reality is that the biggest part of escaping from ropes is just wiggling, which I was doing, but it wasn't easy while lying on my hands. The rough ropes were tearing the skin on my wrists, but I knew it wouldn't matter much longer because according to Timmy's plan, I was only budgeted for fifteen more minutes of life.

Timmy looked down at me and laughed. He might have been an idiot but he knew what I was doing.

"The wiggle thing, right?"

I didn't even look at him.

"Go ahead, Houdini. If you can get out of those knots, you deserve to get away."

I kept wiggling, and wishing he had used handcuffs instead. I heard Timmy giving directions to his comrades. I assumed he was schizophrenic when I heard him talking to them. His personality seemed to snap from gregarious host to concentration camp guard and back again in an instant. While I tried to wiggle out, Timmy screamed and yelled about directions as though his hoods were *trying* to get lost.

He was right about the knots. I couldn't budge them. Then he leaned his big ears back over the seat. Mister Hyde was suddenly gone, and the passive Doctor Timmy was back in his place.

"You're wondering about the ears, right?" he said, without a trace of acrimony.

I said nothing.

"It's because ever since I can remember, I loved going to Disneyland. It's the happiest place on earth, right? I just can't get enough of it. I have a season pass so I can go whenever I want."

I was right. I didn't like the answer.

"You're wondering what my favorite ride is, right? It's the Teacups. Ever since I was a kid, I loved going on those things and puking my guts out."

Then, he just shook his head, smiling and staring off into the distance. He was reliving the memory of regurgitating at the base of the Matterhorn. He looked like a child. A homicidally mad, sartorially conflicted child, who happened to be a serial killer. Then, Mister Hyde suddenly came back, and he resumed the verbal thrashing he was giving his boyz.

I was beginning to think that the best thing to do was go back to sleep. If I've got to go, why bother struggling? Maybe I could sleep through it. But then I remembered what the big dude said, what patches had said, about bringing Jesus the weary and the heavy-laden, and I thought about giving it a try. I was weary. I was heavy-laden, whatever that was. What the hell did I have to lose?

I made a mental note to look up "heavy-laden" if I survived the ride.

While the muffled conversations continued in the seats, I stopped wiggling in the cargo area. Timmy was yelling about where to turn, and I looked up through the back window. I decided to bypass all the Hail Mary's and go right to the man.

"Hey, Jesus, I've never believed in you, but maybe you could help me out of this spot."

I pulled on the ropes. Nothing.

"Hey Jesus, uh, Lord, they told me you would answer my prayers, and I'm asking, praying to get out of this situation."

I pulled on the ropes again. Still nothing. That was pretty much confirmation of my atheistic philosophy, but since I had nowhere else to go, I decided to try it one last time.

"Lord, Jesus, save me please."

Nothing. Damn! I gave up. I looked out the window. For some reason it bugged me. I had never had a problem with walking away from the church.

It was all gobbledygook to me, but for some reason, in that cargo hold, I felt like I was doing something wrong, because I started to feel like God *should* have answered my prayers.

"God? I thought you were praying to Jesus."

"Geeze, didn't you ever go to Sunday School? The Holy Trinity? You pray to God in Jesus' name. Even I knew that."

I decided to give it one last try for the second time.

"Dead God, in Jesus name, I ask to be saved from this situation, and please forgive me for selling my soul to the devil. Amen, Hail Mary, my country 'tis of thee."

I yanked harder on the ropes, and still nothing. I figured if there was a God, I had probably queered the deal by selling my soul, which was ironic, because here I was about to get killed, and still no J. Parnell Thomas, but Timmy's voice was so annoying I had to keep wiggling.

Then something happened. The ropes started to give just a little. I figured it was because I had kept wiggling the whole time I was praying. I started to get a little (you should pardon the expression) wiggle room, and suddenly I was almost out of the ropes. I started looking around for something to cut the duct tape with. I got my hands free about the time the van hit a huge bump in the road. It sounded like we had turned onto a dirt road, and when I moved, I noticed the heavy object bouncing against my ribs was a tool box. Since Timmy was deeply involved in screaming, I felt safe in rummaging.

"Not that way. Stop you idiot, you have to turn right this time! You are soooooo stupid."

The rusty tool kit contained only one item: a Swiss Army Knife. Within seconds, I had silently cut the tape. When I started to move again, every one of my tender muscles reminded me that I had recently been beaten to a pulp, so my first impulse was to lie down again. I had to convince myself to keep going. Timmy started laughing his fiendish, demented cackle, which gave me just the incentive I needed.

I was hoping to open the door latch and slip away without them noticing I was gone. That way I could put some distance between us and maybe find a place to hide, but it would probably only work if the interior lights didn't come on when the door opened. Fortunately, I knew that the interior bulbs very seldom worked in older vans like this one. I popped the door latch and the lights came on. I knew I was screwed. Of all the crummy vans in the world, I get the one where the interior lamps work. I fell out onto the dirt road as the van bounced forward. As I bounced, I understood the true meaning of the word ouch.

I tried in vain to get to my feet. Timmy and his pals must have been a little confused, because the van didn't stop right away, and traveling at speed, it continued about 100 yards down the road. Unfortunately, I couldn't take advantage of the distance because my body didn't want to cooperate.

I got to my feet, and immediately fell over. I tried to get up and run, but my legs and feet wouldn't cooperate. As the van skidded to a stop and the hooligans all hopped out, I finally gave up and started crawling to get out of the road, using mostly my elbows.

If I had been racing a turtle, I would have lost.

Fortunately, the night was completely black. There was no moon out, so I benefited from the cover of darkness. I had been afraid we were in the desert, where I would have nowhere to hide, but we were in the mountains, with a few dark, rustic cabins and lots of trees and bushes in which to hide.

The Timmy gang scrambled back into the van and turned around, with Timmy screaming at his gang the whole time. I managed to get to my feet and stay there as I hobbled on wobbly legs toward the back of a nearby cabin.

As the van raced back, its headlights lit up the entire area, and I fell under a bush just before the lights hit me. Timmy wasn't as stupid as I had hoped, and he parked the van with the engine running, and the lights pointed toward the two cabins, one of which I was hiding behind.

I'm guessing that the only handgun training this motley crew had ever received was in movies and TV shows. Timmy and his two goons all held big handguns like the Charlie's Angels girls. If I hadn't been in so much pain, it might have been enjoyable to watch them pose and point, pose and point. Timmy's gun looked like a Glock, although the model wouldn't really matter if those bullets started perforating my epidermis.

There was a very small chance I could get to the van and drive off, but I would have to go right past these dudes for that to happen. Then, all of a sudden, the lights came on in one of the cabins, and a guy came out onto the porch wearing a bathrobe and a nylon baseball cap with a hunting rifle over his arm.

"What in the hell are you boys doing out there?"

Timmy apparently didn't want to engage in conversation because he stepped onto the porch, pulled the Glock and shot the dude in the throat. While the poor guy squirmed on his own welcome mat, the three hoodlums walked right past him and straight toward me.

These guys were sure to find me. I was hiding behind a bush, and they were about five seconds from tripping over me. I weighed my options and decided to make a break for it. I couldn't get away without alerting them, so my only chance was to lower the odds.

I hoped they would be right on top of me before they noticed me. If they spotted me from a short distance, they would simply shoot up the bush, but if I could jump up and surprise them, (and that was a big *if*) I could stab at least one of them with the Swiss Army Knife. If I could make that longshot happen, an even longer shot was that maybe, just maybe I could get to the other side of the street in the darkness.

The key was to add some confusion to the situation. If I could get these guys flustered, I might be able to get one of the guns, or get one of them to shoot one of his partners.

If I could find some cover on the other side of the road (another considerable *if*) I might be able to make it to the van while the shooters searched the bushes.

I placed my odds at no worse than ten million to one.

Then a funny thing happened. These guys were right on top of me. I mean *right* on top of me. I was even formulating a plan C, whereby they might walk right past me, when suddenly, I heard a shot ring out, then another. Then hooligan number one's head exploded and he dropped like a rock.

"That is pretty funny."

"I told you."

It turns out that the dude on the porch was still kicking, and he was now returning fire. He killed hooligan number one. Then, the dude's wife came out and she had her own rifle. She started popping off rounds and blasted hooligan number two. Meanwhile, Timmy had been blowing away half of the cabin with his Glock, but apparently he couldn't hit anything more than five feet away, so when Ma Kettle turned her rifle on him, he dove for cover.

He jumped over the bush I was hiding under and landed right next to me with bullets whizzing over our heads. You should have seen the look on his face when he realized how close we were.

"I don't know why you didn't think this story was funny."

He started to pull the Glock out from under his chest and I took advantage of the opportunity to stab him right in his good cheek with the Swiss Army Knife. I had never stabbed anyone before. It felt like I was stabbing a steak with lots of gristle. I was actually trying to stick him in the eye, but I was under a lot of stress at the time.

I gave him a couple more shivs to the face and blood was spurting everywhere. He dropped his gun, grabbed his face and started crying like a little girl.

"Not the face. Not again!"

The bullets were still flying all around us and one of them hit Timmy in the shoulder, which made him cry even louder. The shooting actually stopped for a minute, I'm guessing because Ma and Pa Kettle couldn't believe they were locked in mortal combat with such a crybaby.

I grabbed Timmy's Glock, cracked him across the forehead with it and started crawling across the street, according to my original plan. (Except in the original plan I intended to run, and I was barely limping.)

I managed to get to the other side of the road and kept limping toward the still-running van. About this time, Timmy seemed to get his second wind.

"I'm not afraid of you."

While I was wondering if he was talking to me or the hillbillies, Ma Kettle seemed to take umbrage at his temerity.

"You better learn some fear, boy, cause I'm gonna mess you up."

I made it to the van and opened the front passenger door. Fortunately, the driver's door had been left open, so the interior lights were already on. I tried to climb over the center console, but my flesh was simply not willing. It got me into the van and refused to get me any further. I finally decided to speed away from the scene while in a kneeling position in the passenger's leg area.

It's actually a lot harder than it sounds, I was swerving all over the road. I controlled the wheel, throttle and brake by hand. The moment I shifted into reverse and started backing up, the windshield exploded. The Kettles must have assumed I was one of the bad guys and started blasting.

From my vantage point on the floor I was safer, except that I couldn't see where I was going. I decided to throw caution to the wind, pulled up on the emergency brake, yanked the wheel to the left, and managed to do a reverse one-hundred-and-eighty-degree turn. Then the van was pointed straight down the road, away from the battle zone. About that time the rear windshield blew, but I was almost out of range.

Two minutes later, I was at the bottom of the crummy dirt road, and I managed to get into the driver's seat. I turned left onto Big Bear Boulevard, and headed down the hill toward home.

As I coasted down the mountain, my eyes beheld a sight so enthralling, I almost cried. It was a pack of generic cigarettes. I put one in my mouth and searched in vain for a match. The interior lights worked in the crummy van, but the cigarette lighter didn't, so I had to be content with sucking on the unlit stick like a pacifier. It wasn't enough, but it was better than nothing.

While I traveled down the road, I tried to piece together all the elements of this nutty caper, but I couldn't figure out how I was possibly going to emerge from it alive, much less with a completed book. And what about Phoebe? Could I make sure she was okay? And if she was okay, did I feel differently about her than other women I had known? Questions like these were almost enough to make me turn around and let Timmy and the Kettle family finish me off.

Then I saw it.

A row of rustic hotels, each one with a vacancy sign. I pulled the van over to the side of the cliff, climbed out gently, and put the shifter in drive. As the van started over the cliff, I stumbled across the highway to the first hotel, *The Crestview Pine Cabins*. It was a long row of seedy bungalows, and judging by the parking lot, they were all empty.

I didn't want to check in, in case some smart detective might come by later to check on the shootout and the crashed van. So I picked the lock on the very last cabin in the row. I was inside looking out through the Venetian blinds when a huge ball of flame erupted down at the bottom of the cliff. The one, over which, I had just pushed the van.

CHAPTER FIFTEEN
Sanctuary

The cabin was like the Bates Motel, except the shower was smaller, and after wrestling with Timmy I was too tired to worry about Norman Bates' mother sneaking into the room. Judging by the dust on everything, I was confident that I would not be interrupted by a maid coming to clean or even a family from Iowa checking in.

I limped toward the bed, but skidded to a stop when I noticed a beautiful sight: an ashtray, with *Crestview Pine Cabins* printed matches just lying there. Without realizing it, I had kept my stray, unlit cigarette in the corner of my mouth, and while it was now a little dog-eared, it was still a semi-functional smoke. I eased my way onto the bed, careful not to disturb the worn fabric bedspread with cotton beads sewn into the shape of a bucking bronco.

I struck the match and held it to the end of the cigarette. The moment the match made contact, I was filled with delight. The smell of sulfur, the sound of the match igniting, and the gentle crackle of tobacco as it started to burn.

That part felt like foreplay.

I inhaled deeply as the fire trucks started arriving across the highway. I could almost taste the delicious toxic trace metals as I filled my lungs with life-threatening satisfaction.

That part was making love.

I could have done a cigarette commercial at that moment. "My life has been in constant peril and I'm going to hell, but this generic cancer stick makes all of my troubles seem less important!"

I couldn't have cared less about the fire department and the massive attempt to contain the fire in Timmy's van. I knew it was a small blaze that would be extinguished quickly. Ten seconds after the cigarette stub was in the ashtray, I was asleep.

Two days after that, I woke up.

Actually, *woke* is probably too pleasant a description for what I did. My awareness of consciousness was based on pain. Nothing in my experience had ever been as painful as the way I felt that morning. Not basic training, not boxing, and not even the time I listened to an entire campaign speech by Al Gore. I wasn't sure I could move any part of my body, but I gradually started wiggling my fingers and toes. Eventually, I moved arms and legs, but not fast, and not often.

I attempted to focus through the Venetian blinds, but I was blinded by the sunlight. Once the whiteness dissolved and my view became clearer, I noticed a few remnants of police-scene crime tape blowing across the parking lot. There was also a slightly burned row of pine trees lining the highway, but the damage seemed to have been quickly contained. The best surprise was that the hotel staff had avoided checking my room. After examining the dust by the light of day, I wasn't surprised.

It took a full fifteen minutes to get to the bathroom. If Timmy had appeared at that moment I would have surrendered. My movements were small and my strides were short. Once I finally reached the bathroom, I wanted only to turn around and go back to bed.

I spruced up as much as possible, but my face was a mess. My eyes were both black, and the rest of the face seemed to be covered in scratches and bruises. My worst fight in the ring didn't cause this much damage. However, I was slightly amused by what I saw on the bed when I returned. There was an outline of blood in the area of the bedspread where my head had been. It looked like a halo. My white shirt was beginning to look like the Café au lait color favored by J. Parnell, but my black suit was surprisingly resilient. Once I raised my tie into the fashionably loose position I looked pretty good considering what I had gone through.

I didn't realize I had been asleep for two days, and I wanted to get moving before any of the forces chasing me got any closer. I checked out by leaving a couple of singed hundreds on the bed and painfully shuffled over to the diner next door.

The place was called, *Bessie's*, and it was a vision for a guy as hungry as I was. It looked like other places of its ilk, with a log-cabin exterior and a Formica interior. It was tidy, and the elderly waitresses were all dressed in beige uniforms straight out of the fifties, including the lovely matching hats that were bobby-pinned to their graying heads. These women always interest me because they are troopers, controlling their environment with heavy lifting, long after their contemporaries have eased into more secure lives. If you look into their eyes, you can tell they have seen more than their share of heartache, yet they continue to trudge through life, lugging trays of convenience, providing service they will never know in their own experience.

I picked up a newspaper on the way in and was surprised by the date, but not as surprised as when I saw Phoebe sitting in a booth smiling at me.

I tried to look over my shoulder, figuring if she could find me the others must have been right behind, but I couldn't get my head to turn that far. If I could have, I would have seen an empty lot.

Who was this gorgeous chick?

"You must be hungry."

"And you must be a witch. How in the world did you find me?"

She smiled and waved for the waitress.

"Come on, the coppers, the hoodlums, and I can't even imagine who else is looking for me. I couldn't tell you where I am if my life depended on it, yet here you are. How did you find me?"

"You wouldn't believe me if I told you."

"I will believe you."

"You will not believe me."

"I will believe you."

"I'm telling you, you won't."

"I'm telling you, I will."

"The power of the Holy Spirit guided me."

"I believe you--No, you were right, I don't believe you."

She sat there smiling, but I had to admit, even in my pain, it was a great smile.

"Now tell me the truth."

She continued to smile in a way I couldn't resist, then poured some more cream into her coffee and stared out the window. After all I had been through, and as tired as I was, I wanted to take her back to my cabin and ravish her on the bucking bronco bedspread. I hated her and loved her all at the same time.

Wow, did I just say I loved her?

Did that come out of me?

That's heavy.

And scary.

"So what happened? Did you order the number three?"

Well, the waitress was about 85 years old, and it took her some time to get to the table. She was a cute little old lady, and her nametag said, *Hilde*. When she finally got to the table, she took out her pad, touched her pencil to her tongue, and then she looked at us. It seemed like she was summoning all her strength to smile, and finally, the edge of her mouth curled upward so slightly it was almost imperceptible. I wanted to order, and I think Hilde wanted to take the order, but Phoebe was somehow taken with her.

"Hilde, that's a lovely name."

Without speaking, Hilde turned her shoulders like someone with a neck injury toward Phoebe and increased her smile three percent. I felt like Hilde was irritated, but Phoebe must have thought she was growing on her, because she took it as a signal to keep chatting.

"You must love living up here in the mountains."

Hilde's expression didn't change.

"Sometimes I have to pinch myself."

"Me too. Do you ice skate during the winter?"

Hilde turned and looked at me as if to say, "Is she kidding?"

"No, I'm into extreme freestyle snowboarding."

"That's great Hilde. Hey, what do you recommend?"

"I like the French Toast."

"Okay, we'll both have that. Won't we Joe?"

"Actually, I wanted some…"

But before I could tell her I wanted eggs, Hilde was gone. She moved faster when leaving the table.

"Hey Hemingway, the girl said something about the power of the Holy Spirit. What is that?"

"Well, she said it was the power that God gives us to do His will and accomplish His goals."

"So why didn't it work for you in the van?"

"Have you forgotten I sold my soul to the devil?"

"I guess they frown on that sort of thing in the heavenly kingdom."

"Who knows? But I know she made her way up to the Crestview Pine Cabins while you were still down here in town polishing your badge."

"That could be beginners luck, or maybe she had a tip, or…"

"Yeah, I said the same thing when I was looking for a different excuse. I tried like hell to get her to tell me, but that chick is relentless."

Hilde brought our French toast and refilled the coffee. When I looked up from the sugar, Phoebe's eyes were staring into my soul again.

"God is the answer to your question."

"What question is that?"

She shrugged.

"You're the one who has all the bruises."

"You're damn right I know, and I know I have more questions now than when I started this stupid caper."

"God will answer your questions, and your prayers."

"As a matter of fact, I tried that one, and He didn't."

"He didn't what?"

"He didn't answer my prayers."

"When did you start praying? I thought you were an atheist."

"I am, especially now that He didn't answer my prayers. I was in trouble last night, actually a couple of nights ago, and I was so desperate that I prayed, but God didn't answer."

"What did you pray for?"

"I prayed to Him to save me from the kidnappers."

"And?"

"And what?"

"And did you get away from the kidnappers?"

I looked up from my French Toast.

"Well…"

"Did you get away from the kidnappers?"

I though it must have been a trick question.

"Well, yeah, but I got myself out."

"Oh really, you were so scared that you went against your moral beliefs and prayed to a God in which you don't believe, and then you suddenly developed superhuman strength and escaped, aided only by your own perspicacity."

"Well, I don't know if I've got perspicacity."

"Oh, you've got it all right, if you moved the heavens and the earth to escape certain death without benefit of our Lord's blessing, you have definitely been blessed with perspicacity!"

"Hey, calm down."

"Why don't you *make* me calm down? Just use your perspicacity."

She was right; the French toast was delicious, only I couldn't eat it because I was being interrogated by J. Edgar Hoover.

"What do you want me to say? I don't believe it was divine intervention. I need to see more proof before I believe that."

She just sat there staring at me and I just sat there getting turned on by her. With those smoldering hot eyes, luscious lips and great body she was so hot I could have stirred my coffee without a spoon.

"It sounds like you're more interested in her than in writing the book."

"I may be, but it's not because of her looks.

"You just said…"

"I know. I can't explain it. She's got that special, undefinable something, what the old movie moguls would have called, *it*…

"What Christians would call the power of the Holy Spirit?"

"What are you, my Rabbi?"

"I'm a detective. We put facts together, no matter where they lead us."

"Yeah, well I put facts together too, or at least I was supposed to, and so far I had uncovered hundreds of facts that the literary audience would never believe."

Phoebe smoldered for a few more minutes, and then left her untouched French toast plate and stood to leave.

"Come on, I'll drive you down the hill. Leave Hilde a big tip."

I wolfed down as much breakfast as I could. I knew the ride would be arduous, and not just because my bruised kidneys would get bumped around inside her red Karman Ghia. Phoebe hopped into the sporty little car and zipped over to where I stood. She didn't look at me or say anything, so I climbed into the passenger seat gingerly and she took off before I was entirely in. It hurt, and when I say *it*, I mean *my feelings*.

And my kidneys…

and everything else.

On the way down the hill, I was reminded that Phoebe was among the worst drivers in the world. She goes way too fast, rides the brakes, and applies makeup at the most inappropriate times, directing her attention to the mirror when it should be on the road. In the city, this would be one thing, but on a mountain road, it's downright life threatening. We spent more time on the shoulder than on the actual road. After a while, I noticed everyone pulling over and waving us by. By the time we were halfway down the mountain; her brakes were burning so bad that flames shot out the sides of the wheels. The smell of burning brakes permeated the car.

She momentarily turned from doing her lips in the mirror with an uncomfortable expression.

"I can't figure out what that awful smell is. I'm going to take it in to the mechanic tomorrow and have him put on a new muffler."

I was not about to argue with her since she held my life in her hands (along with a tube of bright red lipstick).

Halfway down, we had another surprise. Phoebe adjusted her mirror and gasped. I turned fast, forgetting how painful it was to do so, and saw himself, J. Parnell Thomas, sitting in the Ghia's very tiny back seat.

"Who is that and how did he get into my back seat?" Phoebe yelled.

"Don't worry, he's with me," I told her, before I realized how stupid it sounded.

But J. Parnell himself seemed the unhappiest of us all.

"What is your problem, kid? I promise you first rate information and you don't show up for our session?"

"Hey dude, if you haven't noticed, I've had a pretty rough day, and I wasn't able to be at your session because I was kidnapped, almost killed, and forced to spend the night in a mountain cabin on a bucking bronco bedspread, so back off."

"Okay-okay, just get me one of those what-chamacalits and we'll call it square, but you gotta start getting the story down today, cause you're running out of time."

"First, we're surrounded by pine trees, so you're not getting a Slurpee for at least fifty miles, and second, I'm ready to renegotiate our deal, because I no longer believe it's a fair trade."

"Oh no, you signed this deal in blood. Nobody welches on the Pod, I mean the Prince of Darkness."

J. Parnell looked around suspiciously.

"Did you call him the Pod?"

J. Parnell shook his head.

"POD is an acronym for Prince of Darkness, but he hates that name, so don't tell him I said it."

Phoebe, by this time had heard just about enough thank you very much.

"What in the world are you two talking about?"

"Never mind."

"Is this the girl? Va-va-va-voom!"

Phoebe said, "Hey, I don't do *never mind*. Spill it old man."

She looked at him, he looked at me, and I just shook my head hoping he would keep his big mouth shut. J. Parnell sat there patiently and I thought for once he would help me, and then...

"He sold his soul to the devil."

Phoebe's eyes widened in surprise. She slammed both feet down on the brakes, only nothing happened, they were completely burned out, and the Ghia continued to accelerate down the hill.

"I don't have any brakes. Any suggestions?"

"Yeah, let's go get a whatchamacalit."

"Try to downshift."

She shifted into third gear, and the car slowed down, but then we got a surprise: a truck slammed into us from behind, shoving the Ghia all over the road in a high speed slide. When I turned around to look, I noticed Timmy behind the wheel. He was a mess; his suit was torn and dirty, the scar I had given him was encrusted with blood, mirroring the scar on the left, but the mouse ears were still glowing.

He slammed the big truck into us again and shoved the Ghia right to the edge of the cliff, where Phoebe managed to steer clear of a thousand-foot plunge.

"Okay, so I grew up in New Jersey," said J. Parnell.

"Let's skip ahead a bit."

"How far?"

"To right now. Who is this guy we've got on our tail?"

J. Parnell turned around and noticed Timmy. They seemed to recognize each other. J. Parnell practically jumped into my lap.

"What's he doing here?"

"He's trying to kill us. I thought that was obvious."

"Somebody tell me why he's trying to kill us," said Phoebe.

J. Parnell twisted his face into a confused expression.

"He's not supposed to be working on this case for another week."

J. Parnell slapped his hand over his mouth like a little kid who got caught saying too much.

"Uh-oh."

"What do you mean another week? You knew this guy was going to kill me? You set me up, you lousy creep."

"Did I say another week? I meant another Greek. He's supposed to be hunting a Greek. No a geek. I can't keep track of all the slang you kids come up with."

Meanwhile, Timmy slammed into us again and again, Phoebe managed to swerve away from the edge of the cliff, except that this time, our tires reached the outer edge of the "you're-dropping-a-thousand-feet-to-certain-death zone."

"Come off it, Parnell. I felt sorry for you, but you turned around and fed me to the wolves. I was going to make you famous again."

"I didn't mean to. I was a victim of circumstance. I blame society. It was all Nixon's fault."

"That's the best you've got? Peer pressure?"

"You are really pathetic," said Phoebe.

"You don't know what it's like. I made the deal with the devil to have power back in the forties, but as soon as I got powerful, the Pod, I MEAN PRINCE OF DARKNESS, took it all away, and now I have to rot in hell for eternity while McCarthy gets all the attention. The devil fixed it so no one even remembers me, even after all the souls I sent him."

I looked back at Timmy's evil grin, and the way it looked underneath the Mickey ears. I decided I did want my life to be normal again. I turned to ask J. Parnell what to do, but he was gone, the coward. I noticed a side road coming up and it looked like it angled uphill. If Phoebe could make the turn without rolling the car, we might just live. I put our odds at 500 to one.

"Pull onto that side road."

"Wow, you think we can make it?"

"No, but I'm a pessimist."

I looked back at Timmy, who looked confused, because none other than my pal Jack Kennedy was suddenly sitting in his passenger seat. Timmy was weaving from side to side trying to keep the truck on the road, and Jack was just sitting there smiling at me. He waved, then took another puff on his cigar. I looked ahead and noticed the turn out. I could tell Phoebe was nervous.

"Dear Heavenly Father," she prayed, "Your word says that no weapon formed against us will prosper. I call upon the power of the Holy Spirit to guide us and keep us, and I claim victory over these demons, in Jesus' name, Amen."

Phoebe yanked the wheel; the Ghia rose up on two wheels as it banked across oncoming traffic, around the corner and up the side road. We coasted onto the upgrade on two wheels like a circus stunt, then slowed down and dropped onto all four wheels. I jerked back to see what Timmy was going to do. He was intently timing his turn, but the president calmly leaned over and put his cigar out on Timmy's hand. Timmy suddenly jerked both of his hands up to his mouth and started blowing on the injured paw. He did this for a few moments before he remembered his predicament and re-grabbed the wheel, too late to stop the truck from rolling fifteen or sixteen times before flying over the edge of the cliff.

Phoebe coasted the Ghia over to the side of the road, and finally to a stop. I looked over, and she was resting her head on her arms, which were folded over the top of the steering wheel. She turned to me as if she was going to yell. Then she paused, as if trying to decide what to do. Then she grabbed me and started making with the kisses again. I couldn't figure her out. She pushed me away from sex, but every kiss contained more tongue than a Jewish delicatessen. After a few seconds, I was blissed out by her kisses, and didn't worry about the quandary anymore.

CHAPTER SIXTEEN
The Armageddon Bar and Grill

After a few minutes my already scarred face was blotchy with bright red lipstick. I felt woozy from whatever it was Phoebe was giving me. Suddenly, she looked up at me like she was confused, or frustrated. I looked at her the same way I always did; with desire. Our eyes locked, and I could feel her breath on my face; it tasted like honey.

I never thought much of kisses except as foreplay, but her kisses were somehow important. They said something, and they made me feel like I wasn't such a dog somehow, like I was worthy of the emotions behind her gorgeous eyes. Her kisses were like presents on Christmas morning. I could hear violins playing as I moved in slow motion toward her lips. I couldn't wait to feel her face against mine, and I also wanted to prolong the ecstasy.

And then the phone rang.

"What? What phone?"

"That's exactly what I said, except I was screaming."

It seems the magic phone that Edyth gave me had once again found its way into my pocket and it had the most annoying ringtone I had ever heard. I tried to ignore it, but by this time it was getting hot, so I took it out and tossed it out the window. Phoebe was confused, but I wrapped my arms around her one more time. I was interrupted when I felt something big, like an anvil, hit my shoulder. Phoebe looked up and recoiled. I turned to see a big paw on my shoulder. It was attached to a creature facing me that looked like a cross between King Kong and Mickey Rourke.

The creature wore the by-now-familiar singed ensemble. His was a big-lapelled chalk stripe suit with a large-brimmed fedora pulled low over what I'm assuming were his eyes. Peeking out from under his enormous chin was a tie that displayed a particularly bilious pattern of yellow and green flowers. It was perhaps the ugliest tie I had ever seen, and couldn't have been more appropriate for the big man.

He removed the big heavy paw and held out the phone I had just tossed, still ringing. I reached into his massive mitt and recovered the annoying little instrument.

"Joe Darling," Edyth's voice squealed when I opened it, "you are a very naughty boy. How do you expect to finish the biography when you are running around with dames?"

"Hey, I don't have to take that from you, Cruella. I quit your stupid assignment, and I quit Diablo Publishing. Sue me if you want to, but I'm off the case."

I couldn't stand to look at her, even on a 1.5-inch screen, but I could feel her eyes burrowing into the side of my face, just as I could feel Phoebe's burrowing into the other side.

"Oh no my precious, you will honor your obligation to me and this company. Mr. Mazurki will now take you to a very comfortable place to finish your biography with the honorable Mr. Thomas."

I took a swing at Mazurki, but he just grabbed my arm as it approached his enormous chin and tossed me into the seat next to Phoebe. This dude would have eaten Sasquatch for breakfast.

Then the big guy walked to the front of the car, picked it up like a rickshaw and started to walk forward, pulling the car on two skidding rear tires. After a few hundred yards, Phoebe shifted into neutral, allowing the wheels to roll freely. When the load he was pulling had eased, the big man slowed for a moment, and then slowly looked from side to side as though unsure of himself. He finally stopped, put the car down and turned to face Phoebe. He touched the brim of his fedora and opened his mouth.

"Tanks," he said, in a voice that sounded like a garbage disposal.

Then he again picked up the car and continued, slowly and steadily. However, I got the feeling that something had changed for the big dude.

Another mile down the road was a small log cabin that looked like it had been vacant for twenty years. There wasn't another building in sight, and there were no visible signs of life. A neon sign over the front door was broken and discolored, and spider webs seemed to be the only things that were holding the building together.

Mazurki dragged us to the front of the joint, then gently lowered the front of our German rickshaw to the ground and walked back to the driver's door. Moving deliberately, he opened the door, then took off his hat and offered his catcher's-mitt-of-a-hand to Phoebe. She smiled nervously and stood in her seat. When she placed her tiny hand into his, it disappeared into the large, fleshy lump that protruded from the end of Mazurki's sleeve. His eyes, visible without his hat, were like two shiny black marbles that didn't betray his thoughts, but his actions were gentle, almost courtly. Guiding her out of the car, he behaved like a small boy, awkwardly trying to hold a butterfly without crushing its wings.

About that time another familiar face wearing a singed tuxedo came out the front door swatting at spider webs with the large menus he was holding. He had the familiar broasted attire and skin. He had a pear-shape and large round glasses with large black frames.

The weirdest thing about him was that although there was color all around him, this guy was black and white. Everything about him was in shades of gray, like the special effects on TV. He didn't smile. He didn't look like he had ever smiled. He looked up at the sign, and upon noticing it was dark, slugged an electrical box on the side of the porch. The neon flickered and sputtered, and suddenly became readable in red, green and purple, "The Armageddon Bar and Grill."

"Welcome to the Armageddon Bar and Grill," he said. Phoebe leaned over to me and whispered, "that's Louie B. Mayer. He ran MGM Studios."

"What's he got to do with this?" I asked.

"I guess the movie moguls were also in league with the devil."

"Seems reasonable."

Louie B. started to speak, then simply turned and led us into the grill with his sad-sack expression.

"I have your table ready Mr. McCoy."

Inside, the place looked pretty much like you would expect; dirty, dusty and moldy, but there were also touches of elegance, like white tablecloths, antique silver, and an old busboy who was wearing a short white coat and a very heavy five o'clock shadow. Louie B. held the chair for Phoebe. I didn't pay much attention to the old busboy who held the chair for me.

Singed patrons were scattered around the room, and although no one seemed to be enjoying themselves, everyone seemed at ease. Most sat behind glasses of red wine, with plates of some disgusting appetizers in the middle of the table. No one touched the appetizers, but everyone was knocking back the vino.

Another odd thing about the café was that the inside was at least three times as large as the outside. The place had probably fifty tables, a bandstand, and a large bar at which stood some very creepy, yet captivating characters. I had the feeling I had seen all of their pictures in the scrapbook at the Nix. Everyone had the requisite burn marks, and everyone gave off the sulfur smell that was by that time familiar. But something was missing that I couldn't quite put my finger on. It was like a once-thriving nightclub that had gone out of business, but the customers kept coming.

A five piece jazz combo played soft and low from the stage. They were surprisingly good, employing a mischievous twist to Rossini, but with a jazz tempo. The ghouls in the band all wore tuxedos with varying degrees of burn marks, and their faces showed the now-familiar ravages of the world we had entered. Louie B. handed us menus.

"My name is Mr. Mayer. I'll be serving you this evening. Can I start you off with a glass of wine? We have a nice Shiraz, a Cab Merlot, and some Chianti."

"What about some white wine?"

"I'm sorry, our management doesn't permit us to serve anything cold."

"But it's pretty warm in here."

He shrugged.

"You get used to it."

"We'll have the Shiraz."

"Very good," Mr. Mayer said, and then snapped his fingers like Colonel Klink. "Richard!"

Louie B. left, and Richard stepped forward. Richard was the old busboy I had barely noticed. He swept some crumbs off the table and removed the wine list. He looked like all of the world's problems were resting on his round little shoulders. I couldn't help thinking I had seen him someplace before.

"Does the busboy look familiar to you?"

"Yeah. He looks like somebody I... Oh my God, it's Richard Nixon."

He didn't look like the pictures I had seen at the Nix. He looked like the cartoon caricatures that appeared on the opinion pages during the 1970s. He seemed markedly smaller than the former president, and markedly sadder. Louie B. returned with our glasses and a corkscrew.

"Hey Mr. Mayer, how did Richard Nixon wind up bussing tables?"

"We all have our crosses to bear."

Neither one of us could find the strength to laugh, but there was more to the story.

"Richard's biggest punishment isn't his job, however."

Louie B. snapped his fingers again and Nixon waddled over like a child being called to the principal's office.

"Richard, what do you say when you are addressed by your nickname?"

Nixon just stood there, red-faced and ashamed. He remained silent, and lowered his head even further.

"Richard?"

Again, Nixon the busboy didn't respond. He seemed to shrink even more before our eyes, until Louie B. waved a hand at Mazurki, who was sitting at the bar nursing a juice glass filled with

Chianti. Mazurki stood up and started deliberately toward the former President. Once Mr. Nixon saw Mazurki, he opened his mouth, then closed it, and then tentatively opened it again.

"I am not a Dick," he sputtered in the familiar Nixonian tone.

The whole joint broke into a laugh track. I mean it really sounded like a sitcom laugh track. None of the other ghouls was laughing, but the laughs were in the air.

"I can't hear you," said Louie B., who forced a pinched smile.

Nixon grimaced.

"I am not a Dick," he said, slightly louder.

Then his face convulsed in shame. His jowls seemed to droop to the floor, and he shrunk back into the darkness, wiping his hands with a dirty towel. Everyone in this place was sweating, but Nixon was sweating buckets. I was guessing that this joint wasn't on the health inspector's regular route. As Louie B. fidgeted around the table, the second president with whom I had become acquainted seemed to dissolve into the darkness. His face was a road map of regret that became darker and darker until I could no longer see him.

"So what's the plan, Louie B.? Where's Edyth?"

"She has asked that you start without her. You can begin with Mr. Thomas."

"J. Parnell? Where is the little weasel?"

"I'm right behind you, punk," said Thomas, who was indeed right behind me, sitting at the next table. He sat there like Buddha, and I suspected he was also sitting on some sort of booster seat, because he seemed unusually tall. He was still agitated, but he seemed cockier than our previous meetings. My Selectric and a couple of reams of paper sat on the dirty white tablecloth.

"So what happens now?"

"I'll tell you everything you need to know," said J. Parnell, and then you'll write the stupid book."

"Then what?"

"Then you'll get your best seller and I'll get my legacy."

"No, I mean what happens to me and the girl?"

"You get to be a big famous writer."

"But do I get to be a big famous ALIVE writer?"

J. Parnell looked around the room like he just got caught embezzling government funds, which, apparently he did. I figure this was the expression he used when Drew Pearson blew the whistle on him back in 1948.

"Uh, I, sure..."

For a politician, this guy was a surprisingly inept liar. I looked around the room at all the faces. Louie B., Nixon, Mazurki, and J. Parnell all seemed to have something riding on this deal. I started looking for a way out, and then I looked at Phoebe. She didn't look scared, but she seemed disappointed somehow, in me. I wondered if I could grab her and make it out the front door, but at that point, two more ghouls joined our party. They looked like they knew what I was thinking.

The first one was really beaten up, but dressed like a college professor. Despite the heat, he was wearing a sweater under a tweed jacket. He also wore an ugly tie, and had a handkerchief in his pocket that looked dirtier than Nixon's bar towel. He removed a pipe from his mouth and knocked the ashes into the big ashtray on the table. We may have been at the gateway to hell, but at least you could smoke in there.

The second ghoul was extremely thin. Everything he wore was beige, including his skin tone. He had cultivated a working class hero sort of charisma, and wore round clear eyeglass frames in the style favored by Trotskyites. Tweed Jacket stepped forward, and I recognized him from the Hollywood Ten picture, but I didn't remember which one he was. Trotsky paced behind him muttering like Rain Man.

"You won't make it," Tweed Jacket said.

"Make what?"

"Don't play games. You can't escape, and if you try, he will take it out on the girl."

"Which one are you?"

"I plead the Fifth Amendment."

That was weird. Most of the ghouls, with the exception of Nixon, were very outgoing, but this guy wasn't telling us his name or anything else about himself. I started wondering how intense the restrictions were on these dudes.

"So what am I supposed to do now?"

"Sit down and write the book. That way nobody gets hurt."

Suddenly, Trotsky jumped forward with a loud voice and spastic mannerisms like Barney Fife.

"Oh, you would like that, wouldn't you Dmytryk? Still consorting with the enemy after all these years."

"That's it, Edward Dmytryk. Now I remember you."

"Polonsky you idiot! I'm not consorting, I'm trying to make the best of a bad situation. This is the society in which we live."

"It doesn't have to be. The workers of hell could unite."

Dmytryk shook his head, and Polonsky started marching.

"Arise, you prisoners of starvation! Arise, you wretched of the earth!"

He was marching around a table, holding his knees high. Then he started twitching, which interrupted his song.

"For... justice... thunders condem...nation: A better... world's in, aaugh!

Then he grabbed his chest in pain, gasped, wheezed, and fell to the floor with a thud. Everyone else looked on with disinterest, watching him twitch. Dmytryk calmly packed his pipe, then lit it, then looked up at me.

"As I was saying, you can see the tools which this community has at its disposal. It is futile to resist."

I looked around at Phoebe, and then started walking toward the table with the typewriter.

"Don't do it, Joe. The Bible says that the weapons of our warfare are not carnal. Let God get you out of this."

I turned to her with more sorrow than I have ever known. I envied her faith in God, but I knew better than to go against the machine when a fix like this one was in.

"It's too late for me, baby. Better find another boyfriend."

"No Joe."

I turned to Dmytryk.

"Get her out of here. She doesn't know anything."

Dmytryk shrugged.

"Sure pal."

"No Joe, don't do it. You can't make a deal with these people. The enemy does not come except to kill, steal and destroy. Only God is able to make this right. Joe?"

Dmytryk nodded at Louie B., who nodded at Mazurki, who again reached out his hand for Phoebe, just like the gentleman he must have been at one time. Phoebe slapped it and glared at me. Although her slap barely registered with Mazurki, he lowered his head in disappointment, picked her up and carried her out the door. I turned away and was by this time staring at my glass of Shiraz, but I could feel Phoebe's eyes on the back of my neck as surely as I could feel the buzz that lousy wine was giving me. It was powerful stuff, and after two sips

I needed to sit down. I could hear her yelling and wrestling, but I couldn't look.

J. Parnell leaned his elbows on the table as Phoebe was being removed. She screamed at me all the way to the car outside, where I assume Mazurki again pulled it, rickshaw style, to wherever they were going. I was pretty sure these people would not be honorable enough to actually let her go, but I was positive that I couldn't get her out of this room. My only chance was to bust out of here and then find her.

J. Parnell grinned like he knew something I didn't.

"Pretty strong stuff, huh? Only it's not as good as the whatchamacallits."

"Why did you pad your office payroll?"

His eyes grew wide and he pulled the gavel out of his inside pocket.

"Hey, this book don't have nothin' to do with that stuff. I want to talk about how I stood up to Roosevelt, and how I sent those commies to jail."

This roused Dmytryk's interest.

"Oh, you must be very proud of yourself for that, Mr. Thomas."

"I am proud. Your little commie brothers were sending secrets to the Ruskies and you know it."

"I did not know that. I didn't know any secrets."

"Maybe not, but some of your fellow travelers did. Like your pal Jack whatsisname. I'll bet he knew some things that he wasn't supposed to."

"We've been over this a million times. As soon as I realized that we were taking orders from the Comintern, I gave you the information you asked for. I no longer accepted their ideals and was no longer willing to support them."

"Too little, too late. Now back off and let me tell this kid what to write."

"Yeah, tell me," I grumbled.

"First, this whole business of calling it a witch hunt is wrong. They really were commies and they really were supporting a foreign government."

"So why does everybody remember it differently?"

J. Parnell rolled his eyes downward, as though trying to signal me that something was under the table.

"What?"

He continued with the rolling eyes and started twitching his face downward. At first, the goofy faces he was making made me think he was having a stroke, but then I noticed he was jerking the funny faces downward, almost like he was trying to form a pointer with his face. Sitting there looking at him I decided that he was trying desperately to point downward without using his hands.

"What?"

Suddenly, all the light in the room got brighter, a lot brighter, like I was staring into a searchlight. Eventually, I could only see a big white spot. It was like those movies where somebody dies and they walk toward the light. At the corners of my vision I could make out a few things. All the ghouls reached into their pockets, took out welding goggles and put them on. Of course I didn't have any, so I had to shield my eyes with my hands, which didn't really work.

Next, the front door opened, and an even brighter light, which I would not have dreamed possible, flooded in through the front door. By this time, I was on my knees with my face against the floor. I was trying to shield my eyes by cupping my hands over my eyebrows, creating a sort of dark chamber against the floor, which was totally filthy by the way. Although my face-against-the-floor technique didn't prevent thoughts like, *holy-cow-my-retinas-are-disintegrating*, it did promote thoughts of, *maybe-I-could –still-write-books-on-a-brail-typewriter*.

Then I noticed something else.

It wasn't a noise. It was an absence of noise. Like all the sounds in nature had been sucked out of the room. I couldn't hear music, I couldn't hear conversations, and I couldn't hear my own breathing. I could feel my heartbeat like it was pounding against my eardrums, but there was by that time a perfect stillness, except that the blinding white lights made it seem like the world was coming to an end.

For all I knew, it was.

The air was completely still and completely silent, but there was a painful, oppressive presence in the room that seemed to pressurize the atmosphere like we were inside a balloon that was about to pop. Then I realized that it wasn't bright white at all. The room was in fact completely black, but it was a black not found in nature, a darkness that burned so brightly it was impossible to look at.

And it hurt.

I couldn't see how the ghouls were reacting, but I was in a lot of pain. My whole body felt like it was being squeezed, and not in a good way.

Then I heard what sounded like a horse walking across the floor toward me. It was definitely some sort of clippety-cloppety, like hooves. "Why would they have a barnyard animal inside their club?" I wondered. From what I could tell, everyone else in the room was down on their knees, and bowing their faces to the floor as the animal approached. I struggled against the glare to look up, but couldn't. From my vantage point on the hardwood, I finally made out what looked like horses' legs wearing a pair of tailored slacks. Those slacks stepped into the spot on the floor right in front of me, but I had bigger concerns. My legs ached, my back ached, even my tonsils ached, and they had been removed when I was nine.

But wherever they were, I knew they were throbbing with pain.

I had my hands over my face, I was undulating like Rosie Perez, and I burst into tears. I cried like a baby. It was the closest thing to relief I could muster.

Then I heard the voice.

"Please don't struggle to look up," a booming voice said, "it will do you no good, and leave you with quite a headache."

Booming, isn't really an adequate description of the voice, but it's the closest I can come. The voice seemed to take up all the empty airspace that the sounds had left behind. Now my ears hurt worse than anything else, but the sound was so powerful it seemed to bounce off my sternum. I noticed I could plug my ears with my thumbs while my hands were covering my face. I looked idiotic, and I felt even worse.

The voice was right. My head already ached like never before. I kept my hands and thumbs in position and turned away.

"I heard you were looking for me," the voice boomed.

My ears rang like gongs, my head ached, and I couldn't believe I was hearing this expression again. This had to be the Pod, except I was too terrified to ask, so I fell back on my usual cockiness.

"I don't know who you are."

"I am known by many names. You may call me your Majesty."

"So what makes you think I'm looking for you?"

"Because you have taken such a keen interest in certain members of my staff."

His voice, if you could call it that, was pounding away at my eardrums. It hurt to listen, and I couldn't take it. Even when he stopped talking, the voice continued to bounce around the room with the torque of a locomotive. I couldn't take it another second, and without realizing it, I decided to take a chance.

"Get to the point, would you?"

Then, it sounded like an atom bomb had exploded and I was in the middle of it. It was so loud I didn't see how I could take any more of it. Something really bad had happened and everybody knew what it was except me. I wasn't prepared for what happened next. I was terrified but tried not to show it. Then, a horrible realization occurred to me.

The Pod was laughing.

Except, it wasn't like any laugh I had ever heard. It was so loud and powerful that everything in the club started breaking, exploding, and otherwise falling apart. Lamps erupted in a shower of glass and whatever else they put in those things. Glasses shattered and came raining down over me. Plates, cups and wine bottles were all broken up as the laugh pounded against my brain. I could feel the floor shake. I was hit by flying glass and other shrapnel. Then there was one big thump and everything, including me, bounced up and down in synchronization. I can't be sure, but I am guessing that the Prince of Darkness slapped himself on the knee.

Then, as the laughter died down, I began to add up the factors involved in my situation. First, although it was a little hard for an accomplished atheist to wrap his psyche around, I had to recognize that the devil existed and was in the room with me. Second, what the heck did he want with me? From everything that had happened so far, I figured it had to be about this J. Parnell book, but why did the devil care about setting the record straight on the blacklist? Third, is this guy really happy with me in a, I-like-this-guy-and-I'm-going-to-let-him-and-his-girlfriend-go, kind of way, or is he just laughing like Lee Marvin in an, I'm-so-evil-I-get-a-kick-out-of-toying-with-my-prey-before-I-kill-it, kind of way? I was pretty sure I knew the answer to that question, but I didn't like the way it fit when I tried it on for size.

Finally, the pressure on my ears was lessened and I noticed a loud ringing inside my eardrums like a civil defense drill. Meanwhile, every inch of my body, inside and out, felt like it had been run over by a tank.

"You are funny," the voice boomed.

For once in my life, I had no desire to crack wise with a witty retort. I just laid there.

"You made me laugh, so here's what we're going to do. First, you will write the book with Shorty here. Second, you will go on a promotional tour with Edyth, and she will show you the ropes of our organization, of which you will become a valued member for as long as you are of use to me."

Then I waited for the third requirement, but heard nothing. Finally, I couldn't take it any longer.

"And third?"

"Third is whatever else I want. I haven't decided yet, but I'll think of something."

He gave off a little chuckle, which didn't do too much damage, but still rocked the whole room back and forth. I made a mental note to never make this dude laugh again.

I was convinced that I was fighting an unbeatable enemy, and not only that, I had already signed over my soul to him. Just like when I joined the Army, I was obligated, committed, stuck. But unlike the Army, my hitch was going to last forever.

"You've got my contract."

"Glad to see you're a stand-up guy. Not like most of these losers who tried to weasel out of their agreements. Hey, did they show you the Nixon thing?"

"It was very humorous," I said with as much sarcasm as I could muster. My ears still screamed with his every syllable.

Then I felt a Buick land on my shoulders.

It pounded me into the ground with such force that I don't know what kept me alive. The pain was unbelievable. "How can I possibly still be alive with this much pain?" I wondered. Then I realized that my face was pressed directly against one of the hooves.

"Oh, I get it. It's not your kind of humor."

I had definitely cracked wise with the wrong dude this time. I made a mental note to never speak again.

"That's okay. I'm easy to get along with, as long as you do everything I say. Now kiss my hoof and we'll be friends again."

At that moment, I was somehow awake to hear the man say *ten*.

I was not brave. I kissed his crummy hoof like I was engaged to it.

"You didn't."

"I did."

Then the excruciating darkness went away and people started moving around again. The ghouls took off their welding goggles and I did an inventory of body parts to see if anything still worked. To my surprise, although the pain lingered, I was able to get to my feet with only minor difficulty. I sat at the table, took a big gulp of the Shiraz and stared into J. Parnell's pinchy little face.

CHAPTER SEVENTEEN
And Then I Ran For Congress

Thomas sat on the other side of the dirty tablecloth waxing poetic about his years on the hill. From time to time he would surreptitiously stick his head under the table quickly and then bring it back up with a smile on his face. A glance under the table confirmed my suspicions; he had a Slurpee stashed under there. As to why he had it hidden, he would probably have had to fight for his life if the other ghouls spotted such valuable cargo at the Armageddon.

I was listening to the miserable little loser drone on about what happened after Drew Pearson *framed* him.

"Wait a minute. You can't say you were framed because you admitted you did it."

"But everybody was doing it. You punks don't realize that politics is about taking everything you can steal until the other guy gets caught, and then you crucify him for it."

"Only this time you were the one who got crucified."

"That doo-doo-head Pearson. It's his fault, and he only got wise because one of my old girlfriends tipped him off."

"So you were also an adulterer?"

He looked at me with an, *are-you-kidding*, expression.

"Oh please, they should put in it the oath of office that you're gonna screw around while you're in Washington. It doesn't mean anything. The fix is in. You hire your girlfriend as a secretary, and then her job is to keep you happy. It doesn't mean you don't love your wife, it just means you love the fringe benefits too."

His words hit too close to home. What had happened to me, I wondered, that his speech now made me want to punch him? This guy had the same moral values I had built my life on, and I hated him for it.

"So tell me about prison."

"Can you imagine? I'm in prison, and fifty other guys doing the same thing on Capitol Hill get to keep livin' it up."

"So why didn't you blow the whistle on them?"

"I made a deal."

"Who did you make a deal with?"

"The same guy as you."

"And he wouldn't let you blow the whistle on the others?"

J. Parnell started getting nervous. He cleared his throat, looked around, and then shook his head.

"That's enough. Next subject."

"Why can't you tell me?"

"That's enough. Next subject."

In J. Parnell, I saw a guy who wanted to tell me, a guy with no self-control, a guy who should be telling me.

But a guy who wasn't talking.

He was plenty scared, and I knew why. I was pretty scared myself.

Then, I noticed Nixon enter my field of view, slouching in the shadows. Slowly, the former president stood erect. He seemed to gain back some of the demeanor he had in the pictures at the Nix. He stopped staring at the floor and made eye contact with me. He very calmly gestured for me to meet him in the kitchen. He was a different man now. He was calm, covert, and even presidential.

"Where's the bathroom?" I asked J. Parnell.

"What? Oh, it's over there, through the kitchen."

J. Parnell ducked under the table for another Slurpee fix and I got up and walked past Nixon, who continued to clean a dirty ashtray. I walked into the kitchen and there stood my old pal Jack Kennedy. He had a big smile on his face and a Slurpee in his hand.

"Hey Soldier, I ah-understand they gave you a pretty hard time. Let's get out of here."

"We can do that?"

"Of course we can."

"Isn't there like a force field or something?"

"Na, this guy is too cheap to install that sort of technology. He-ah maintains he's omnipresent, but we know better, don't we Dick?"

"I am not a... oh, yeah."

"I love this guy. People don't realize he was the one friend the writers had on the HUAC panel. Even then, he knew how to work for the just while everyone thought he was working for the politically expedient. In the end, he usually accomplished both. See you outside Dick."

"It's pretty surprising to see you hanging out with Dick Nixon."

"Did you know we came to ah-Congress the same year? We had both been Navy Lieutenants in the South Pacific. Our offices were right across the hall from each other."

Jack turned to leave and I followed. We walked out the back door and I expected armed guards all around the place, but there weren't any. I looked back at Nixon. He quickly ducked into an alcove and emerged in a crisp black suit. All vestiges of the busboy had vanished and he now looked more like the active President than the hunched-over ghoul. Jack saw me watching him and stood over my shoulder.

"One of the best parts of eternal life is that I have been able to rekindle my friendship with the gentleman from California."

"You two were friends?"

"Sure. Didn't you read Chris Matthews' book?"

"Huh?"

"I recommend it. He did a good job of showing that originally we were essentially the same guy in terms of government, but it all fell apart in 1960."

"Was it because you ran against each other?"

"I suppose so. We both did things of which we would later be ashamed, and pretty soon that was all we did."

Nixon then emerged from the kitchen to hear Jack's comments.

"My friend Jack is right. The world might have been a very different place if neither of us had run for president. But the good news is that God has redeemed our friendship and we get to work together once again."

Nixon then extended his hand awkwardly toward Jack, who clasped his right hand around Nixon's, while holding them together with his left hand. The two legends locked eyes and smiled. I felt distinctly like a voyeur intruding on a private moment, until Nixon broke it up.

"We better hit the road before they get wise to us.

Kennedy winced.

"I keep telling you Dick, you can't pull off the vernacular.

"Really, I thought I got it that time."

"Let's talk about it in the car."

From the outside, it was the same deserted cabin I saw when we arrived. Jack was driving a beautiful, red 1950 bullet-nose Ford convertible. It looked like it had just come off the showroom floor and smelled like it too. We hopped in and he hit the gas. The car was flying down the mountain road in seconds, and Jack skillfully bobbed and weaved with the road. He turned on the radio and Peggy Lee was singing, *Why Don't You Do Right?* Then he started singing along with it.

"You had plenty of money in 1922,

You let other women make a fool of you."

I just sat and watched him. Here we were probably about to get blown up at any second and he's singing Peggy Lee. He seemed as happy as a clam, rocking back and forth as the trees whooshed by outside his door.

"Why don't you do right,

like some other men do?"

I looked to Nixon to become the voice of reason, but he started singing as well.

"Get out of here,

get me some money too."

His familiar baritone murdered the lyrics, but both of them were having fun.

"You're sittin' down and wonderin' what it's all about.

If you ain't got no money, they will put you out.

why don't you do right,

like some other men do?"

"So what happened back there? How did Mr. Nixon change sides?"

211

"He was with us all along Soldier. The Lord had him working as a spy in the Pod's camp; a double agent. Cool, right?"

"Wow. How long were you there?"

"Since I died in 1994."

"Man, that must have been tough."

"Well, I always knew this day would come, and that I would get to see my wife again. Although it's especially gratifying that Jack was here to meet me. I…"

Nixon stopped. Neither Jack nor Dick looked at each other, but both seemed to be fighting back tears. I made a mental note to read that book.

"So how does this routine work?"

"Well, the Lord has a few more guys like Dick stashed behind enemy lines to help characters like you."

"How?"

"Uh, characters stupid enough to go into business with the Pod. He hates that name by the way."

"I heard that."

"The Pod is a lot worse than you could imagine. When I grew up we were naturally scared of him, but people aren't scared of him anymore, and they don't find out how dangerous he is until it's too late."

"Yeah, I saw."

"You didn't see anything, kid. This guy's potential to kill, steal and destroy is unlimited. There's only one power that's greater."

"Good?"

"God."

"So where is God if he's so powerful?"

"He's right next to you Soldier, and has been every step of this trip."

"Then why did he let the devil beat me up and kidnap my girlfriend?"

Wow, did I just call Phoebe my girlfriend? I continued to be surprised by the depth of my feelings for her.

"God didn't let the devil beat you up. You did."

"I did?"

"I know you don't think you did, but the lesson will have to wait until we get your girl out of this joint."

He pulled the car over in front of another ramshackle cabin and the three of us jumped out of the car and barged into the cabin. The place was as disgusting as I would have imagined. Her Ghia was right in front of the place, but Phoebe wasn't there, and neither was Mazurki.

But his suit was.

Jack motioned for me to take a look in the bedroom, and I could see Mazurki's chalk stripe lying on the floor in three inches of purple goo. The walls had been sprayed with the goo and the windows seemed to have been blown out by the explosion. I looked at Dick.

"What happened?"

"He must have tried to help the girl."

"Help her?"

"Yeah, he didn't really have the heart for this line of work."

Jack sat down dejectedly in the living room.

"Well, I don't know what to do next. Mazurki was my last clue."

But Nixon would not hear of it.

"Wait a minute. We can't just quit. We've got to look around."

"What are we looking for, a monogrammed keychain that says, *Lucifer*?"

"Maybe. Give me a minute."

"Make it quick. The cleanup crew should get here pretty fast."

I looked around the room. She had been here all right. I could see the footprints of her high-heeled boots in the dust on the floor. She had obviously been stomping around while they waited. She wasn't what you would call patient.

I went back into the bedroom where Mazurki's remains oozed through the cracks. Something wasn't right. His clothes were all around the room, but two things were missing, his horrible necktie and his fedora. I looked in the other rooms, but couldn't find them. Jack was in a hurry.

"What are you looking for?"

"His hat. It's not here."

"Maybe whoever took her, took the hat."

"I don't think so."

Both presidents continued looking around, without success. I got the urge to stop looking and just stand there in the center of the room.

"Hey Soldier, we must make hay, and we

must do so with great vigah! They will be here any minute."

I closed my eyes and let myself listen, in case someone was trying to get in touch with me.

"Okay Lord. Do your thing."

Almost immediately, I heard something inside my head say, *attic*. I looked at the ceiling and saw the attic access. I pulled over a rickety, ladder-back chair, stood precariously on it and pushed the attic cover away. Once I stuck my head through the opening, I noticed Mazurki's fedora was sitting right at the edge.

"Let's go Soldier," Jack yelled.

I grabbed the hat and ran for the door. Jack had the car revved up and right outside the front porch. I jumped off the porch, into the Ford, and away we went.

The Hummer came out of nowhere, drove right past the cabin and roared after us.

It looked exactly like the Hummer I had dispatched in Yorba Linda, and was equally impossible to see into. The Yorba Linda Hummer was trying to get away from me. This one was trying to get me.

Jack maneuvered beautifully on the Mountain road while Dick quietly observed. The car seemed to glide around the banks, completely under control, but at tremendous speeds. The Hummer was equally adept at negotiating each curve, and carried the added menace of its huge size, bearing down on Jack's beautiful convertible. In spite of this, Jack was again listening to his Peggy Lee songs. Apparently, these guys know an all-Peggy Lee station.

In the excitement, I had forgotten about the hat in my lap. I looked in the hatband to see if she might have slipped a note inside of it, but there was nothing. I turned it over to look inside, still nothing. Then, I opened up the disgusting sweatband inside the hat, and inside the sweatband, in bright red lipstick, Phoebe had written, *Timmy*.

I showed it to Jack, who seemed to brighten even more.

"Well, why didn't you say so? I know where to find that punk."

Suddenly, our windshield exploded.

I looked over my shoulder, and I noticed one of the Blinkers with the green skin and red eyes. He was strapped to the roof of the roaring Hummer on a platform, and on that platform was an anti-aircraft gun like you used to see on the deck of battleships in World War II movies. This Blinker looked like John Belushi in the Samurai costume, but he was wearing a German helmet with the sharp point at the top. He was firing the big gun at us, and everything else in sight. Although he was belted onto the platform, the Hummers movements were jerking him all over.

So as the Blinker fired at us, he was blasting trees, other cars, birds, and other assorted non-targets in a motion like a pendulum. He sprayed large caliber ammo to the right when the Hummer swerved left, and vice versa. If we had been on a straight road, we would have probably been destroyed, but the curves allowed us to calibrate the path of the bullets, and duck when we saw the shells start coming back in our direction.

Then I noticed the Blinker screaming in his little munchkin voice. This one sounded exactly like *Cousin It* from *The Addams Family*. Every time he would miss us, we would hear more screaming and yelling that sounded like munchkins on a killing spree, which, I guess, this was.

After two more misses, the Blinker exploded into a purple haze. It looked like a mini version of the death star exploding over the Hummer, then covering all oncoming traffic with the gooey, airborne Blinker remains.

As soon as the smoke cleared, an identical Blinker climbed up, tried to strap in, but was thrown overboard by the violent motion. He exploded in midair over a minivan carrying a frightened soccer team. A third Blinker then climbed up, successfully strapped in, and took over operation of the big gun. After two more misses, he too exploded.

"I've got an idea," said Jack.

At the next turn, he barreled a hard left into a little town called, *Forest Falls*. He shoved his foot down on the throttle and was probably doing a hundred miles an hour down the main street of the town. We charged through the sleepy little hamlet with the Hummer in hot pursuit, shooting the heck out of Main Street and the convertible.

By this time we were on a fairly straight road, so the latest Blinker's aim was better. Jack, Dick and I were all riding low in the seats, but the

Ford dashboard by this time looked like a range target. Jack zigged and zagged, and managed to gain some ground on the Hummer, heading toward a tunnel that had been carved right through a small mountain at the end of town. We hit the tunnel at top speed, and Jack slammed on the brakes, skidding to a stop just inside the entrance. The Hummer picked up speed, coming after us.

"Jump," said Jack.

It sounded crazy, but I jumped. Dick stayed in his seat, but looked angry when he saw me standing next to the car.

"Run," he yelled. "Get lost."

I took off running in the darkened tunnel, but it wasn't dark very long, because the Hummer slammed into the Ford and both cars exploded. Two of the Blinkers staggered out of the Hummer. They were on fire for a moment, and then exploded into a spray of purple goo, which, by that time, was flaming purple goo.

The fading munchkin screams narrated their own demise as their molecules rained down over the area and was a surprisingly beautiful sight in the setting sun.

As the fire continued, Jack and Dick were standing next to me, seemingly none the worse for the explosion. We had to run to the other end of the tunnel to get out, and at the other end, a yellow cab power-slid to a stop in front of us. I followed Jack into the back seat. The cab peeled out and I relaxed, until I saw the driver.

"Patches?" I asked in disbelief.

"Man, why would you call me patches?"

"Well, you seem to be wearing a lot of Patches."

"Yeah, but that ain't who I am. That don't define me."

"I'm sorry. What is your name?"

"My name is *Patch*."

I tried for, but didn't get any sympathy from Jack or Dick.

"Guys, this is…"

"Hi Patches," they said in unison.

"Don't you two start with me."

Suddenly it was like I was with the Freshman Class of 1947 and these two were the big jokers. I finally figured out what was bothering me about this picture.

"Uh, Patch, aren't you blind?"

"Yeah, so what?"

"Well, how are you driving the cab?"

"I ain't drivin' this cab. The Lord is drivin' this cab. He's just using my hands and feet to do it. Ain't you never heard of the power of the Holy Spirit?"

"Well, yeah, but…"

"See, that's why people can't use the power; because they doubt the power. God fills us with the power if we ask him. If we have the faith, we can move mountains. How tough can it be to drive a car compared to movin' a mountain?"

"So why don't you use the power to cure your eyesight?"

"Are you kiddin' me? Then I might have to watch reality TV."

"Okay, so where are they?" asked Jack.

"I'm on my way," Patch responded.

"Don't you both think I deserve to know what the heck this is all about?"

"Okay, but a smart guy would have figured it out by now," said Jack. J. Parnell Thomas brokered your soul in return for a best-seller, right? Except the book was never going to happen, because that's the Pod's ah-modus operandi. He gets your soul in exchange for something shiny, but in the end, you go to hell and don't get the shiny part either."

"Yeah, but if I was to give the devil his due, I would say that he did set me up with J. Parnell, and I would have eventually finished the book."

"Then why is he chasing you around this beautiful resort community with an anti-aircraft gun?"

"I don't know. Why did he have J. Parnell dictating his story to me, filling in the blanks?"

Nixon then turned to me with a stern expression.

"Listen Junior, Do you think you're the first blacklist nut he's lured into damnation? That period has been a recruiting bonanza for the Pod."

"That was just a stall to get you in position."

"Position for what?"

"So that *you* have to go out and start bringing souls back with you."

"No way. I would never do that."

Jack and Dick just shook their heads.

"Everybody does it kid. You can't stand up against that guy. You got just a hint of what he's really like. He could have you swindling souls in under five minutes."

"I would kill myself first."

"You would already be dead, Soldier. That's why Timmy's trying to kill you and not Phoebe. She's saved by grace, so the only way she could go to hell would be to renounce everything she's lived her life for."

"Okay, there you go. She would never do that."

Patch leaned over the front seat toward me with an expression just like the Mother Superior's. He continued to steer without *looking*.

"She might do it to save you."

That hit me in the gut. I suddenly realized that making a mess of my affairs didn't just affect me, it affected the only woman I had ever loved, and I hadn't just ruined her life, I was on the verge of ruining her eternity.

"What can I do?"

"Yeah, we gotta get her back from Timmy and kick some serious bounty hunter ass!" Patches injected.

"Bounty hunter?"

"That's right," said Jack. Timmy is the devil's top bounty hunter. It's his job to knock off the slobs who sell their souls so they can't enjoy their shiny stuff."

221

"He works out of Anaheim, and I know he seems stupid, but he's relentless. He has all the power of the dark side at his disposal, and he waits you out. He doesn't stop until you're rotting in the Lake of Fire."

"So how do we beat him? Can we set off one of those purple explosions?"

"Nobody sets those off except the Pod. The little guys with the red eyes are all on a sensor. Once they lose their effectiveness, they blow up automatically, but Timmy is a different story."

Patch nodded.

"The only way Timmy can get blowed up is for the Pod to do it his ownself, and he's gotta be there to make it happen."

"I thought he could just make it happen, like by remote control."

"Weren't you listening? Only God can do stuff like that because only God is omniscient. If you want the devil to blow up Timmy, you must make the devil pretty darn unhappy with him, and he has to be right there to see that."

"So what's the plan?"

"I'm glad you asked."

CHAPTER EIGHTEEN
The Showdown

It was raining hard when we pulled off the Golden State Freeway at four in the morning. Patches had turned over the controls when he got tired and was now sleeping in the back seat, piled up with Jack and Dick like three toddlers returning from a night at the drive in. Dick and Jack both had their faces resting on Patch's chest, and all three snored. They sounded like hibernating bears.

The cryptic directions Jack had given me involved exiting at Harbor Blvd. Now that we were here, I hoped to learn what it was all about.

"Here we are gentlemen."

A thin line of drool descended from the corner of Jack's mouth, which was very surprising from such a debonair personality. It wasn't pretty when all three sputtered to consciousness, but it didn't seem to bother them that I had seen them like that. I guess when you've seen the stuff these guys have, it's tough to be shocked.

"Now tell me why we're here in Anaheim?"

"Take a look to your right, Soldier. What do you see?"

I looked up and saw nothing but a huge green fence, and then I looked a little higher and saw some trees. A little higher than that, I saw what looked like the side of a mountain, which seemed unusual in the middle of a city block. I realized exactly where we were once we passed a short term parking lot, because I saw an enormous incandescent sign that read, *Disneyland: the happiest place on earth.*

"Of course. Why didn't I think of it?"

"Hang in there Soldier. We'll make a detective out of you yet."

It stopped raining almost the moment I pulled into the Disney lot. We dumped the cab in short term parking under a sign that said all violators would be towed, and started running toward the front gate.

"But it's four in the morning. How do we get in?"

"Hey, we're supernatural beings. You think we're going to-ah have any-ah trouble with Disney security?"

"You're right."

"But *you* might."

"What?"

"You might have trouble getting past security."

"Can't you just pull me in with your magic?"

"It ain't magic, Soldier, I keep telling you, it's the power of the Holy Spirit."

"Okay, so power me in with you."

"You must learn to do this for yourself."

"But Phoebe's in there."

"So you better start learning fast. I told you that you can move mountains, and they've got a mountain in there."

Just then, an electric golf cart with two security guards pulled in front of the three of us. I stopped, but Patch, Dick and Jack kept moving toward the iron front gates, which were eight feet tall, and locked. I knew why the guards ignored those three, but it was really beginning to get on my nerves. The old dudes were by that time morphing through the thick gates as though they weren't even there. Then I stopped wondering and started listening to the big guard who was yelling at me.

His name was Gabriel. I knew that because he had a prominently placed nametag with *Gabriel* engraved under a drawing of Mickey. Gabriel wasn't happy that I had breached security in his sector. I stood there looking for an entrance while Gabriel tried to implement proper security procedures.

"Sir, I must ask you to leave the area. Sir, you are trespassing on private property. Sir, the police have already been called and you will be arrested if…"

He stopped talking when I started running.

Gabriel and his partner ran after me shouting into their walkie-talkies. Gabriel was huffing and puffing while trying to work his radio.

"We have a rabbit! Two officers in pursuit towards the main entrance!"

Gabriel and his buddy were both winded and having difficulty running and talking. I was pretty sure I heard one of the radios hit the concrete, but

225

I wasn't curious enough to break stride. Heading toward the gates, I seemed to be approaching a dead end, until I spotted a bench, under a fence, under the roof of a building where you check out strollers and wheelchairs. I made a mad dash for the bench, using it as a step, then I hit the top of the fence in one jump, and was on the roof of the wheelchair building in two.

Suddenly I was back in Afghanistan. I felt that special wind beneath my wings and I felt great. It was like I made the leap onto that truck when I was downrange just to prepare myself for this moment.

My adrenaline was really pumping at this point. I found myself wondering how my life might have been different if I had thought of running like this when I was being arrested in the Reno library. Then I thought about Phoebe and what I would do to that punk Timmy if he hurt her.

I sprinted across the building's nice flat roof. It was actually built into the side of a berm on which the railroad tracks were built. It seems the Disneyland Railroad passes right over the building. I know that because I tripped over one of the tracks and hit the ground with an extremely uncomfortable crack, just before I heard the recorded voice of the Disneyland announcer chanting, "all aboard!"

Once I recovered and crossed the tracks, I saw a very well lit Main Street on the other side of a fifteen-foot drop. Actually, *well lit* doesn't begin to describe Main Street. This place, sans tourists, was genuinely magical. The lights were all lit and the music still played. The bright lights still beckoned as during operating hours, but now the invitation was much more intimate, like a siren's song.

But I decided NOT to go toward the light.

Security forces were assembling on Main Street, and I could see a backstage area behind the buildings that reminded me of the Universal Studios Tour. Backstage seemed to be a much more sensible option.

Standing on top of the berm, I saw a roof that was probably a twelve-foot jump from where I stood. I knew I had long-jumped 25 feet in high school so how tough could this be? I was pondering that question when a squad of security officers ran toward me. Without further consideration, I ran back to gain some momentum, then ran forward and leaped over the twelve-foot chasm that separated me from the officers and the roof. I felt pretty good as I took off, and continued to be optimistic for about eleven feet. Then I became aware that if I made it at all, it wouldn't be with my feet. I reached out with my hands and grabbed on for dear life. I hit the roof with a thud, landing on the edge of the roof, on my chest, and knocking the wind out of my lungs. I was hanging off of the edge with my legs dangling as I tried desperately to catch my breath. The police and security squad below grabbed at my feet, and with no wind in my lungs, those guys seemed to grow larger by the second.

I made a mental note that competitive long jumping would be much more interesting if the jumper was being chased over a fifteen foot drop, or maybe a tank filled with sharks. Anyone who made it over that would *deserve* a gold medal.

I managed to pull myself onto the roof, considered lying there for a moment to catch my breath, then ditched that idea when I heard ladders clanking against the wall next to me.

I got to my feet and started running tentatively over the roofs that lined Main Street. They took me about halfway down the street where there was a gap of about forty feet between buildings. I knew I couldn't make this one, but some workers had run one of those big orange extension cords from a pole on top of the far building. A swarm of coppers was closing in and I didn't have time for good sense, so I grabbed hold of the cord and jumped into the air, hanging on for dear life. I was using the cord like a Tarzan swing, but it's a lot harder and scarier than it looks in the movies.

Amazingly, the cord held me as I flew out over the abyss. I quickly realized that I wasn't going to land softly on the other building as I had hoped. I was instead going to slam into the side of it.

People don't realize the pendulum effect of swinging 40 feet. By the time I hit the wall, it felt like I must have been going sixty miles an hour. I was dazed and confused, but the voices of the swarming herd of coppers brought me back to consciousness.

I felt like I was back in the ring.

Once your bell has been rung by a solid punch, you can't just call time out. You have to soldier on, stay on your feet and hope your wits will come back to you. After hitting the building, I was so stunned I could almost hear the referee counting, but I grabbed onto the cord and climbed up the wall with my feet like I was conquering Mount Everest. I made it to the top and no one was around, so I ran as fast as my drowsy state would allow toward the other end of the building.

I noticed the rooftop cops who had been chasing me all had to turn around and run back to their ladders because there weren't any more extension cords for them to use. That gave me a few seconds of a lead. I ran until I ran out of roof, and from there I looked up at the big mountain I had seen from the street, the Matterhorn.

If you've ever been to Disneyland at night, you know that every night, Tinkerbell flies off the top of the mountain all the way down into Fantasyland. It's not too hard to spot the wire that she rides all the way down, but it's a great stunt, and since she's 194 feet in the air, it's not for the squeamish.

When I looked up at the Matterhorn that night, I knew immediately what Timmy had done, because I saw Phoebe, the woman I loved, hanging from the Tinkerbell wire, 194 feet off the ground, and struggling to get loose.

I could also see Timmy's golden mouse ears reflecting the park lights from below. He saw me and waved me over like we were old friends. I couldn't see his evil smile. I could feel it.

This really got me hot. My head cleared, my face reddened, and I was anxious to meet up again with my old nemesis.

I was hungry for some hitting.

I jumped onto a fire escape and barely used it on my way down. From there, I could see the cops closing in, but they didn't even worry me. I was hungry for hitting.

I ran past an outdoor restaurant, through a well-manicured park that lined the hub in the center of the park, and I saw the green iron fence that surrounds the man-made mountain. A hoard of police and security personnel closed in on me, but I wasn't worried because I knew something they didn't. I ran toward the green iron fence. Next to it sat the cleanest trashcan I had ever seen. I used a park bench and the aforementioned trashcan to repeat my two-step jump onto the top of the green iron fence. I leaped to the other side just like I had done in Afghanistan. Colonel Hardin would have been proud.

From there, I ran under the monorail to the sloping base of the mountain and started scrambling upward. I was a little out of my element at this point, and as the mountain got steeper, I got slower.

The good news was that there were a lot of folds built into the concrete walls of the mountain. I could use them to climb. The bad news was that I was, by that time, about fifty feet off the ground. I remembered I wasn't all that crazy about heights. This was compounded by the fact that somehow, rocks were now falling all around me, banging off my hands and head, and generally making for a very uncomfortable distraction.

Unlike my last time hanging from a high place, I didn't have amorous neighbors to take my mind off of my circumstances. I also wasn't drunk, but I found most of the courage I needed when I looked up at Phoebe dangling from the wire.

By this time, Phoebe had almost stopped struggling, which I didn't think she was capable of doing. She was hanging from the wire, dangling by some flimsy cord that was tied under her arms and over the Tinkerbell wire. I didn't know if she might suffocate or lose consciousness in her current predicament, or if I would in mine.

By this time, I was probably a hundred feet off the ground, and experiencing an almost constant rock shower. The staff had a searchlight on me, but they stayed at the base camp outside the green iron fence. I guess they figured it was a wasted effort to chase me up when I would probably fall to my death at any minute. I assumed they hadn't yet spotted my girl or the demonic bounty hunter who was torturing her. I kept climbing, and by the time I was halfway up the mountain, I could hear Timmy's voice.

"Hey loser, come on up."

"Hey loser, I can kill her at any time."

"Hey loser, you are gonna be dead the minute you get here, and then I will kill your girlfriend too."

He wasn't subtle, but he was definitely in charge. About that time, I started to wonder about Dick, Jack and Patch. Why weren't they doing something? I mean, I wanted to save her, but I could have really used some help. Then, for some reason, I wondered if I would even be able to get down if I did rescue her.

"Stop it," I said to myself. I didn't have time for the *what-ifs*. I kept climbing, but the grooves seemed to get a little less groovy as I got higher. I figured I was about 125 feet up, and I was really getting tired.

I made the mistake of looking down, and when I did, I slipped. I was hanging by the fingers on one hand. I had somehow grabbed a little security camera while my other hand and both feet hung out over the abyss. Well, actually they hung over a sloping concrete mountain and miles of the cleanest sidewalks I had ever seen.

The crowd below grew so large it looked like it was waiting for Elvis, or Mickey. I took my eyes off the *certain-death-if-I-see-it-any-closer* view and turned to face the *my-one-true-love-is-in-mortal-danger* view. I managed to find a foothold, then continued my climb.

"Ooh, don't fall. Then I wouldn't have the chance to kill you," Timmy said while hurling rocks in my direction.

This guy was really beginning to annoy me.

Then, in my legs, I felt the same burning sensation I had experienced when I fell over the balcony on that first night. Then I felt the burning on my arms, and when I looked, I spotted a big nasty Blinker, hanging on my knee with his fangs locked into my thigh.

I instinctively smashed him against the mountain. He made a lunge at me and I shoved his face into a concrete bump--painted to look like snow. The moment I did, he exploded. The force was like hitting the water face first and I was blinded by the purple goo that covered me. When I got my eyes a little clearer, I noticed there were two more Blinkers, one on each leg.

But there was something familiar about these two.

I soon realized they were Leo and Melvin.

The two leg breakers were now Blinkers, and they looked like they were in a really bad mood.

"Not laughing now…"

"Are you tough guy?"

"You can run…"

"But you can't hide."

I had to hand it to them. They had perfected their call and response technique, but somehow I imagined there was something more menacing in store. They both sunk their fangs into my calves. I grimaced in pain. Man that hurt. I could hear their *Cousin It* voices gleefully narrating their evil deeds, and they kept alternating muffled versions of, "etcetera, etcetera, etcetera."

I managed to kick Leo off and I could hear his munchkin scream all the way to the base of the mountain. I wondered how many times I was going to have to kill this guy.

Then I turned my attention to Melvin and kneed him into the mountain, but he wouldn't budge. He just kept screaming munchkin etceteras. I shook my leg trying to get him off, but that didn't work either. The pain was excruciating.

So I tried a different approach.

"Hey Melvin, How did you wind up in my drier?"

He looked around and started talking, but his voice was muffled because his whole mouth was sunk into my leg. He released his bite and smiled.

"That little Weirdo in your apartment…"

"J. Parnell?"

"Yeah. I came over to shake you down and he answered the door."

"What happened?"

"He had about twenty Blinkers in the living room. He made them grab me and start shoving me into the dryer."

"I'm guessing it was painful."

"Only 'till I died, and then it got more painful. You can't believe how much it hurts in hell."

"So why are you here working for Timmy?"

"Because we will take any job to get out of hell for even a second."

"I'm sorry to hear that, Dude."

"Thanks, and I'm sorry about biting your leg."

"Any chance we could sort of forget this part?"

"No way man. He'll send me back."

"Did you know there's a 7-Eleven on the corner?"

"So?"

"So you could get a Slurpee while I finish off Timmy."

Melvin looked around to see if anyone was watching.

"Well, I guess no one will notice if..."

Suddenly, Melvin exploded in a shower of purple goo. I felt a little guilty, but I had one less distraction.

Then a new Blinker bit me in the butt. I couldn't get him off, but I got an idea. I released my grasp on the mountain and fell. As I fell, the Blinker's eyes got wide in terror, and the little weasel let go of me and grabbed onto a ledge. After I fell past him, I grabbed onto *his* feet.

The little creep actually managed to hold on for a few moments. He let out huge *Cousin It* grunt when my weight yanked on him. I figured his arms were probably stretched by the force, but under my weight, he soon lost his grip and fell. As soon as I felt him fall, I was able to grab onto the mountain again and re-start my trek back to the top.

I heard the Blinker bounce and roll all the way down. It was a series of ugly, painful grunts and cries that culminated when he blew up all over the green iron fence.

I started making better time. When I was about twenty feet away from the top, Phoebe could see me, and I think she started to get hopeful, but she didn't look good. When I got closer, I could see what was holding her up, the particularly bilious pattern of yellow and green flowers of Mazurki's tie. Somehow, it looked even uglier than the last time I had seen it.

I knew I needed a better approach than the one I was on, because Timmy was in perfect position to ambush me. I started looking around, but I couldn't see anything that looked promising.

I began to negotiate my way around the mountain, but that route was even more precarious than the direct approach, and would take lot longer to travel. I also knew that Timmy would have no trouble following me around and ambushing me when I reached him. He had certainly found a perfect spot for this, and for the first time in my life, I worried about losing a fight.

About that time, Patch came climbing along the side of the Matterhorn like a mountain goat. Somehow, he moved effortlessly, while I clung precariously to my position. His white cane hung from the strap on his wrist, rattling as he went. And while the rocks from Timmy continued to careen off of my cranium, they all missed him. Go figure.

"What are you doing here?"

"Well, I can see you cain't save this girl all by your own self."

"I agree. Why don't you get up there and take care of this situation for me?"

"Boy, how many times I got to tell you that I don't do anything? The Lord works through me."

"Well, then get the Lord up there and save her. She's a Christian and everything. This should be a no-brainer."

"But that ain't the way it works."

"Then tell me how it does work."

Just then, another Blinker came scrambling toward us. This one looked like Dewey, but it could have been Louie. I had other things on my mind. Patch didn't hesitate. He simply held his hand up in Louie/Dewey's direction.

"In the name of *JESUS*, be gone."

Louie/Dewey exploded. Patch did a half-turn toward me.

"Cool, huh?"

Then he continued as though he had just swatted a fly. As the rocks continued to fall around us, and I hung perilously from a ledge, Patch got comfortable, leaned against the cliff and folded his arms across his chest.

"In the book of Second Chronicles, the army of Judah was a-marchin' on a place called Mount Seir. It seems those Seir-ians had turned away from the one true God and was worshippin' their own little gods."

"Great story. Now, can we rescue Phoebe?"

He ignored me and went on with the Sunday school lesson.

"But there was a problem. Judah's army was heavily outnumbered, outgunned and out-everythinged, but they was right with God. Well, these soldiers they started to sing."

"To sing?"

"That's right."

"What did they sing?"

"They sang praises to the Lord."

"Like what?"

"Like, 'give praise to the Lord, for He is good, and His mercy endures forever'."

"And?"

"And they just kept singin', 'give praise to the Lord, for He is good, and His mercy endures forever,' all the way to Mount Seir."

"Okay. So what?"

"So when they got there, a funny thing happened. All them Seir-ians was dead. The speaking of God's name and praising Him was what won that battle."

I just looked at him like he was crazy.

"So you want me to...sing?"

"Maybe."

I didn't like singing, and I didn't believe the story, although I wanted to. I just hung there on the wall, until...

"Joe!"

I looked up and it was Phoebe. She was calling me, and it sounded like she was choking on the stupid necktie. I looked at Patch again, then I turned my face toward her.

"See, she's a child of God, but she's putting her faith in YOU right now, so you gots to put your faith in *God*."

I didn't have time or energy to think. I had no choice but to believe. I started moving up the mountain just as a torrent of rain started falling, and since I was willing to try anything I started to sing.

"All praise to the Lord for He is good, and His mercy endures forever."

My voice sounded rough and squeaky, but I looked up to see if it worked. I looked into the storm and saw Timmy grinning and waving at me, as though my singing didn't seem to bother him a bit. Then I heard Phoebe again.

"Joe, please!"

I turned to Patch in frustration.

"Come on Dude, you gotta leap into the fray here."

"It don't work that way, son. You gots to do it. Walk by faith, not by sight!"

I started climbing, but I knew I was outmatched. This was way over my head. If I was going to get her out of there, I couldn't chance depending on my own abilities. I had to do it his way, so I believed God could subdue the bounty hunter with my singing.

"All praise to the Lord," I squawked while struggling upward, "for He-ee is goo-ood, and His mercy en..., ouch, dures, for-ever. All pr-AISE to AAAH!"

I found myself sliding down the soggy mountain and I ripped my hand on a jagged piece when I grabbed it to stop my fall. "Enough, already," I thought to myself. I had lost about ten feet, which I now had to make up, and I was going to do it without singing.

Concentrating on climbing without music, I made better time, and I got to the top in just a few minutes. When I pulled myself onto Tinkerbell's launching pad, I saw Timmy off to the side, lying in a heap.

"Woah," I said to myself. "The praise must have worked." Then I turned my attention to Phoebe. She was barely conscious and about fifteen feet out on the wire. I wasn't sure what prevented her from sliding down the wire, and I also didn't know how to get her back. I looked around for a rope or something to get her, but couldn't find anything. I would have to fix this problem the hard way.

I was wearing my canvas Army belt. I took it off and threw one end over the top of the wire. Then I buckled the belt and pushed it in front of me. I grabbed onto the wire with both hands and started climbing, hand-over-hand to Phoebe.

My plan was to pull her back to the top, but as soon as I was 194 feet off the ground, I realized I had two Blinkers hanging from my waist, and they were trying to climb up my torso. This was horrible. The little weasels were a lot heavier than they looked. I tried to shake them off, but nothing worked. Then they did something really nasty.

They started tickling me.

I thought I had seen crummy behavior before, but that was the lowest. The little monsters were tickling me. I can't take that crap, and I was this close to letting go just so I could take them with me. Then I remembered the singing.

"Ha-ha-ha-all praise to the Lord, for He is good HA HA, and His HA HA mercy endures for HA ever!"

And that was all it took. The two Blinkers looked at each other and erupted into a munchkin, "NOOOOOOOO!" They both exploded while hanging onto my waist. The explosion hurt, but the lighter weight felt good. I climbed over and pulled Phoebe toward me.

Then I turned to see Timmy standing at the top with a big gun. He displayed his usual nasty smile, which made me unusually queasy.

I put our odds at no worse than two billion to one.

"Idiot," he said to me. "I was almost dead when you stopped singing, but I'm feeling much better now. You didn't have faith, and now it will cost both of you your lives."

I just looked at him. Had I come all this way and defeated all my opposition to be killed in the happiest place on earth, taking my dream girl with me? Then all of a sudden, Patch tapped his way right past Timmy and climbed hand over hand out toward us. I think Timmy was so stunned that someone would wander into the line of fire; he didn't know what to do. Patch was blocking Phoebe and me from Timmy, although that wouldn't last long if the punk started blasting.

"Okay boy, this is the moment where you gots to step up and be a man. You gots to accept the Lord Jesus as your personal savior."

"Can't I do that later?"

Timmy aimed the big gun at us and pulled the trigger. Patch said, "Jesus," and the gun jammed. And it stopped raining. I just hung there, stunned.

"Boy, unless you let Jesus save you from the Phillistines, you ain't gonna have no later."

Timmy removed the clip, checked the ammo, put the clip back and pulled the trigger again. Patch, without looking said, "Jesus!" Again, the gun jammed.

"But don't I have to live a good life first? And don't I have to…"

"Boy that's *WHY* we accept Jesus, to forgive our sins."

A frustrated Timmy pulled the trigger five times in quick succession, with no success, and no bullets.

"But I sold my soul to the devil! I signed the contract in blood."

Phoebe and Patch, even in their perilous surroundings, found my statement so humorous, they both started to laugh out loud. I couldn't believe they could find anything funny in this predicament.

"What?"

Patch just leaned over toward Phoebe.

"Maybe you can talk to him?"

"Joe Honey, that stuff doesn't matter when you ask Jesus into your heart. Your sins are all forgiven. No matter what you did."

"But isn't the blood on the contract binding?"

They laughed again.

"Ain't no contract wit' da Pod that the Lord cain't render null and void!"

After examining the gun, Timmy aimed it in the air and fired successfully. The crowd of officers down below all flinched. Patch leaned his head back toward the heavens and yelled, "praise Jesus!" Then Timmy tried again to shoot us, but the gun started Jamming again.

I couldn't get started. I knew I needed help. Somehow Patch sensed it and leaned in toward me. I looked him straight in the eye that was closest to me.

"Help me."

Patch suddenly seemed completely calm.

"Oh, Lord, please forgive me…"

I closed my eyes, which wasn't easy, and repeated Patch's words.

"Oh Lord, please forgive me…"

"And save me from sin…"

"And save me from sin…"

"From this day forward…"

"From this day forward…"

"I call myself a Christian."

"I call myself a Christian."

"In Jesus' name…"

"In Jesus' name…"

"Amen."

"Amen."

I was dangling on the wire, hanging on for dear life, and Patch started singing "Softly and Tenderly Jesus is Calling," just as he had been when I first saw him on the street.

"…Earnestly, tenderly, Jesus is calling, calling, oh sinner, come home."

The words to the song suddenly meant more. They meant everything.

I had turned my back on Jesus, lived a hedonistic lifestyle, abused everyone who ever got close to me, and Jesus was still calling out for me; wanting to give me his salvation. And hanging on a wire, 194 feet above the ground, a guy can use a lot of salvation.

Then I heard a voice. I thought it was inside my head, but now I know better. It wasn't mysterious, and it didn't have sound effects. It was as clear to me as anything I've ever heard. It sounded like someone standing behind me had spoken over my shoulder, but there was no one behind me, 194 feet in the air.

"I heard you were looking for me," the voice said.

I freaked out a little bit. I wasn't freaking because I didn't know who said it. I was freaking because I did.

It was the voice of God.

I know what you're thinking, but I also know what I heard, and God spoke to me while I was hanging on that wire. He told me I was forgiven, and that He had a place for me in His kingdom.

I heard, "I give you my blessing."

"I forgive your sins."

"I love you."

Then I opened my eyes in time to see Timmy climbing hand over hand out to where we were. He knocked Patch off the wire, and at that moment, the necktie holding Phoebe snapped. I grabbed Phoebe, and when I looked down, Patch was spinning and falling like the overhead shot in a Hitchcock movie.

I hated myself for being weak, but I had to save Phoebe.

I hooked my elbow through the belt. She fell into my grasp and wrapped her legs around my waist. Timmy let go of the wire and grabbed onto my shoulders, trying to pull me off. Their combined weight seemed enormous, but somehow I hung on. Then suddenly, we started sliding. The added weight started us on the long slide that Tinkerbell made every night just before the fireworks. Except I was pretty sure this wire wasn't built for three people. The wire sagged as we were speeding along on it. I could smell my belt burning up from the friction.

We went even faster and I tried to shake Timmy off, but that wasn't happening. Phoebe shoved her thumb into his eye, causing him to squeal, but he didn't let go. By this time, Phoebe had both arms around my shoulders, hanging on for dear life. As we passed over the teacups, I remembered what Timmy had told me on our first meeting, how it was his favorite ride.

"Hey look, teacups!"

I didn't expect it to work, but Timmy looked down. When he did, I gave him a left jab that was once described as "nasty" in Sports Illustrated. Timmy lost his grip on my pants and fell at least 175 feet. I looked back in time to see him land directly on the short metal fence around the teacups.

He should have broken in half, but he got up and started running away.

I wasn't prepared for what happened next.

It seemed like there were thousands of birds in the trees surrounding the mountain. I know that because all at once, they all took off in a single migration. It was like a Hitchcock movie. Once the birds had gone, I felt the same absence of sound I had experienced at the Armageddon Bar and Grill, like all the noises had all been sucked away.

The sky lit up like it was daytime, and the same painful, oppressive presence was pushing up against me like those plastic bubbles they use to pack stuff, just before they pop between your fingers.

I knew what it was and I didn't like it.

The Pod was in the house.

CHAPTER NINETEEN
The Chase

I didn't know where Timmy was running, but I was pretty sure he couldn't outrun the Prince of Darkness. He took off in a panic that belied the fact he had fallen 175 feet and landed on a steel railing.

Then the sounds came back, as did the darkness. The birds started appearing, and the oppressive heaviness seemed to vanish.

I had almost forgotten that we were still sliding down Tinkerbell's wire, approaching the landing area in Fantasyland. We got a terrific view, but my arms felt like they were ready to explode by the time we finally passed over a black wall and I could see the landing area, a large foam bag like the kind pole vaulters use to cushion their fall.

Twenty feet before we reached the bag, I was beginning to think we would actually land softly in the bag, but just then my Army belt finally snapped and we dropped like rocks. We fell about fifteen feet and both landed feet first before bouncing around on the concrete. I managed to get up, and except for sore feet, seemed pretty normal. Phoebe's ankle, however, was badly hurt, and she couldn't walk. I carried her over to the foam-filled bag and laid her on top of it. She put her arms around me and just stared into my eyes.

"What?"

She continued to stare, without saying anything. I could see her loveliness through all the dirt and grime that, like me, had been attracted to her. It was just like the first time I noticed her beautiful eyes.

"I really got it bad for you, Baby."

"Nice grammar from a writer."

We started to kiss, but then the bag next to her head exploded and stuffing flew everywhere. Someone was shooting at us, and I knew who it was. I yanked her unceremoniously behind a small metal dumpster that sat nearby and covered her with my body.

The air was suddenly wild with bullets ricocheting off the dumpster and clanking around the area. I peeked from behind the dumpster to see Jack walking around the corner toward us. He had that familiar walk with his right arm raised as though he was about to stick it in his pocket, and he was not at all concerned about the gunshots that were raining all around him.

The shots faded into the background about the time he reached us.

"What are you doing back there Soldier?"

"Didn't you notice the gunshots?"

"Yeah, he's gone. I've got a car out back."

I jumped up and followed Jack, but her voice turned me around.

"Take me with you."

When I saw her I was stunned. She was crying. All throughout this adventure, she had been such a tough cookie, and now she was making with the tears, and that was hard to take. The truth was, I didn't want her to go where Timmy could hurt her. I wanted to go off and be a hero for her.

"No way, Baby. This time I finish it."

Then I ran around the blue wall and saw Jack, sitting in the front seat of a brand new Crown Vic sipping a Slurpee. Dick was sitting in the back seat making Nixonian tones over his frosty treat.

"Ooooooh that's good."

As I passed behind the car, I noticed the words; *Police Interceptor* mounted on the trunk. I jumped into the driver's seat and was about to hit the gas when I noticed something caught on my shoelace.

It was a hat: Timmy's golden mouse ears.

The special, limited edition, Fiftieth Anniversary model golden ears. I tossed them in the back seat and aimed the Crown Vic.

"What happened to Patch?"

"He's going to look after your girlfriend."

"But he fell off of… oh never mind."

"Where were you when I was hanging from the wire?"

"We've got other customers you know."

I had just pulled onto Ball Road when a yellow Checker Marathon cab smashed into us from behind, spilling the Slurpee all over Dick's lap.

"Now this guy is getting on *my* nerves."

Dick recognized the problem.

"The Pod saw you embarrass him. He's dead unless he can turn you back, and quick."

"Turn me back?"

"Yeah, when you accepted Christ as your savior back there, you cost him a customer, and now more people know about the loophole."

"So he just wants me? Not Phoebe?"

"Both of you. Otherwise, whatever is inside of him will explode all over Orange County."

"Then let's see what he's made of."

Then, just as Jack was about to sip, Timmy slammed into us again, and this time Jack flew off the handle.

"Okay, Punk, that's just about enough of that. Move over Soldier, I'm taking the wheel."

"No way."

"Move it Pal. I haven't been this angry since my P.T. Boat got rammed in the South Pacific.

Jack, who had been the picture of composure throughout this adventure, suddenly started wrestling with me for control of the steering wheel. Still holding the Slurpee, Jack was shoving his way across the bench seat, pushing his foot toward the gas pedal, and grabbing at the wheel. I was getting freckled with red Slurpee and had a supernatural being around my neck. I half expected Jack to explode.

So I reached out my finger, fighting Jack's grabs, pushed my arm to the radio and pressed the only button I could reach. Peggy Lee's voice came on singing, *The Way You Look Tonight.*

"Some day, when I'm awfully low,
when the world is cold…"

Almost immediately, Jack relaxed and eased back into the soft leather seat. Then he looked at me and shook his head.

"I'm sorry, Soldier. I thought I-ah had gotten over my bad-ah temper. I guess the boss isn't done with me yet."

Nixon wasn't paying attention. He was singing.

"I will feel a glow just thinking of you, and the way you look tonight."

I hit the gas and started singing myself. The next thing I knew we were all singing, which must have looked pretty weird to Timmy.

I bobbed and weaved through traffic as the rising sun peeked over the Matterhorn. I zipped over to Manchester and was on my way downtown. Timmy was on my tail the entire time, so I started formulating a plan.

But first, I remembered something Patch had told me, that I had to learn to do it myself, so I turned to my mentors.

"Why don't I meet up with you later?"

When they looked at me, they knew exactly what I was doing and smiled with pride.

"Excellent Soldier. And by the way, it's good to have you with the organization."

Jack and Dick both vanished from the front seat and I made a hard left on Lincoln Avenue.

I had driven past a beautiful little alley the previous night on my way to the Magic Kingdom, and I thought it might provide the perfect spot for us to end our little spat.

CHAPTER TWENTY
I Told You Not To Stand There

Almost everything about Timmy was super. He was strong, fast and ruthless. His weakness was with strategy. I suppose The Pod considered it a liability to allow his demons the ability to reason. As a result, Timmy had lightning fast reflexes, but he couldn't figure out what I would do next.

He was bandaged over most of his face and head, with dried blood all over his imitation designer suit and a deadly expression on the parts of his face left uncovered. He had no trouble keeping up with me when I was driving in a straight line, but he spun out of control just about every time I turned a corner. When that happened, Timmy was unable to control the cab and he would wind up stalled in the middle of the intersection or on someone's lawn.

Good drivers are always under control. The vehicle is like an extension of their body. They bob and weave, cut between speeding cars, and slide the vehicle around corners easily. Bad drivers tend to sideswipe and bump every other vehicle on the road, and they rarely make a corner at speed without spinning their car three or four times and having to start the chase all over again. Timmy wasn't a great driver, but his physical power meant that I couldn't make a single mistake if I hoped to beat him.

I saw his face before I lost him in the streets around Disneyland. The bandages couldn't conceal the murderous look in his eyes. He was crimson with fury, and his suit looked like one of those sections of the Berlin Wall.

There was a lovely, open pack of Lucky Strikes sitting on the dashboard. I pulled one out and placed it between my lips unlit. I savored the smell for a moment, but I didn't light it. I was saving that.

After I zipped down a back alley, Timmy couldn't make the turn. I could have made it all the way to Canada, but I needed to end our little quarrel, so I spotted a couple of cops writing a ticket for some poor schlub.

I parked the Crown Vic across the street from them, pulling behind a rusty Plymouth, then stepping out and leaning against the front fender facing north by northwest. That way I had a perfect view of the intersection where I lost Timmy.

Within a few minutes, I saw Timmy's cab fly though the intersection. He spotted me about halfway through and slammed on his brakes. The massive tire squeals got the attention of the cops, who must have thought they hit pay dirt, ticket-wise. Timmy's Marathon continued to slide through the remainder of the intersection and out of view. Next, I heard his tires squealing in reverse as he backed up and into the intersection again. The cops did a silent double take toward each other as Timmy turned menacingly toward me and sat in the intersection revving his engine.

His car continued to make that vroom-vroom-vroom sound like a kid playing with toy racecars. That sound seemed to make the coppers nervous, as this might not be your *run-of-the-mill pull-over-and-cite*. Of course that meant they might, as a consequence, have to arrive late at the donut shop. As a result of all the vroom-vroom, the cab was genuflecting like a bull facing a matador, scratching his paw in the soft earth of the arena. Both cops placed their hands nervously on their holstered weapons.

I pulled my right hand out of my pocket. It was still bleeding and wrapped in a bloody rag. I made a mental note to find some first aid at my earliest opportunity. Then I grabbed a big wooden match out of my jacket pocket and extended my arm. As the cab continued to scratch at the earth, I smacked the red tip of the match with my thumbnail and experienced the violent flash you only get from the big ones.

Instead of lighting my Lucky Strike, I reached into the car and pulled out Timmy's golden Mickey Mouse ears. I looked him straight in his freaky little eyes and held the match up to the ears, which ignited like a Roman candle. I couldn't hear him over the sound of his engine roaring, but I could see him screaming at me. Then I made it worse when I leaned over and lit my cigarette on the flaming ears. I could see Timmy go postal. He pounded his hands on the wheel, and bounced up and down on the seat of the undulating cab. His eyes grew wide and the cab peeled out, heading straight for me.

I inhaled deeply and dropped the remains of the flaming ears into the gutter. I think it might have been the most rewarding smoking experience I ever had. I let all the delicious tars and resins penetrate deep into my lungs before exhaling smoothly.

Ordinarily, it would have been disconcerting to realize that all of Timmy's rage, not to mention a two-ton cab, was hurtling toward me, but this time I was all for it, because I knew something he didn't. When Timmy was about twenty yards away from me, I stepped calmly out of his path. At which point, Timmy realized he was going to miss me, and he couldn't compensate in time. This made him panic, and he slammed on his brakes, which sent his cab into a violent spin.

It seems Timmy hadn't noticed that the previous night's rainfall had left a huge puddle in the middle of the street. Timmy was at the epicenter of the puddle when he decided to hit the brakes. The two cops abandoned their traffic menace as the cab spun wildly. By this time, it was like a deadly Frisbee hurtling toward my car. It seemed like slow motion, with the cab spraying waves of rainwater as it hurtled toward the inevitable collision.

Since I was safely out of the crash zone, I was able to enjoy my cigarette and watch the show.

When the cab smashed into my car, it brought everything back into real time. The noise was the first thing I noticed. The impact made an audible crunch that was probably heard blocks away. The force shoved both vehicles onto the sidewalk and halfway across a well-manicured lawn, leaving grooves in the turf that looked distinctly like varicose veins. After that, the sights, smells and sounds all seemed to mingle as everyone and everything began to react to this horror.

I wandered over to the wreckage and grabbed Timmy by his cheap lapel, dragged him unceremoniously over the steering wheel of his pre-air bag vehicle, and plopped him down on the street with a noise like the sound you hear when you accidentally knock a steak off the barbecue and it hits the concrete patio.

I felt completely invigorated. I was on familiar turf, yet I knew, even while it was happening, that I had been changed.

I had grown.

I was now different. I wasn't better, but I was now forgiven, and the power of the Holy Spirit was enabling me to beat the crap out of this satanic bounty hunter.

Timmy seemed to snap out of his slumber, and when he saw me his eyes grew wide with anger. I closed them with a right-handed punch that was once described in an Army magazine as *thundering*. Timmy was knocked out after one punch, but I kept hitting him just in case. I hit him again and again, and each punch seemed more enjoyable; for me anyway. I had never felt the urge to hit anyone as much as I felt toward Timmy, and I have to say I was truly disappointed when the cops pulled me off of him.

The coppers quickly had Timmy and I bending over the hood of their cruiser. I noticed the familiar click of handcuffs snap twice. If you've never been handcuffed, you might not realize how uncomfortable they are. Some cops (like these two for instance) enjoy going the extra mile and really grinding them into your wrists. This ensures that you are going to feel a great deal of pain when you wind up sitting on your wrists in the back of their squad car. But before they could get us to the car, a funny thing happened.

The cops looked at each other with a sort of smug expression. You could see that they were quite proud of the way they had handled this crisis, even if it had fallen completely into their laps. They were barking orders at us in that particular vernacular practiced by coppers. "Don't move," and "freeze," and probably half their vocabulary dedicated to prohibiting movement, but I doubt that Timmy was listening. I know I wasn't.

I wasn't worried about the coppers because I knew something they didn't. The lights got bright, the birds flew out of the trees, and the sounds all disappeared. Then Timmy's eyes rolled back and he started shaking violently. It looked something like a seizure, but with a little extra nastiness thrown in for good measure. Timmy was shaking with every part of his body, his eyes seemed to be rolling around like slot machine cherries, and smells were coming out of him that I was sure these cops had never smelled before. I knew the cops wouldn't listen to me, but I leaned toward one of them anyway.

"Officer, I wouldn't stand so close to that guy if I were you."

"Shaddup," he said, searching for his keys to unlock the handcuffs. With their attention fixed completely on Timmy, I took a few covert steps and ducked down behind the rusty Plymouth.

And that's where we came in.

CHAPTER TWENTY-ONE
Genesis

I sat there looking at Detective Jones, who had removed his jacket and rolled up his sleeves. The color had all drained from his face. He looked like he had lost his best friend, twice. I reached for another Lucky Strike, but I had emptied the pack. Dick's eyes were watching something far away. He opened both hands and lowered his face into them. Then he wiped his face vigorously, as though he might somehow be able to wipe away the elements of this drama.

When he removed his hands, I was still sitting in front of him. He shook his head like he had been hoping it might have been a dream.

I knew that feeling well.

Finally, he stood up and paced back and forth a few times. I watched him as he went back and forth, then he leaned forward, placed both hands on the metal table without a protective guard and looked directly into my eyes.

"That is the biggest load of crap I have ever heard in my life."

I said nothing.

"Crap, I'm telling you. *CRAP!*"

I remained silent. After all, I had told him at the beginning of our story that he wouldn't believe me.

Finally, he took out his handkerchief, wiped his hands and walked to the wall phone. He removed a pencil from his shirt pocket, used it to punch numbers into the phone on the wall, and then to punch the *Hands-free* button. When the phone at the other end picked up…

"Yes sir?"

…he leaned toward it.

"Bring those reports in here."

Then Detective Jones used his pencil to disconnect, and continued to face the wall, keeping his back to me. I could see his reflection in the two-way mirror, and at that moment, I knew that he was in torment. He understood what he had to do and it was killing him.

Then it got really *really* weird.

I realized that I wasn't concerned with how his decision might impact me.

I wasn't worried.

I remembered what Patch said about walking by faith and not by sight, and somehow I just knew that this was going to turn out well for me.

Did I actually have faith? I never saw that coming.

The two coppers who arrested me came in, wearing clean uniforms and bandages. They put the reports on the table, and Jones turned and picked them up. Then he faced the coppers like a general saying goodbye to his troops.

"You two didn't make this collar, you didn't ever see this guy, and you didn't ever give me these reports. In fact, you've never seen me before in your lives."

They looked at each other, and then nodded to Jones. The cockiness was all out of these guys now. When they left, Jones walked over and caught the door with his foot before it closed behind them. He put the reports under his arm, his hands in his pockets, and scooted the door back open by pressing his back against it. Then he stood holding it for me.

"Get out."

I knew good advice when I heard it. Jones was looking at the floor when I passed him, and I wanted to say something.

I even had something in mind.

But I couldn't do it.

I was halfway down the hallway when he called out to me.

"What was the name of that church you went to?"

I turned and noticed another guy who was no longer so concerned with looking tough.

"The Rock."

He looked back down at his shoes.

"I, uh, may have to check it out to make sure your story, uh, you know…checks out."

I just nodded, smiled, and turned to go, but something stopped me. I remembered the beautiful golden Zippo lighter in my pocket. I took it out, turned and tossed it to Detective Jones. Then he nodded and smiled. I turned again, and made my way out of the building. I had experienced pain as never before during this adventure, but somehow, at that moment, I had never felt better in my life.

It was a beautiful, sunny day when I came out of the station. It became more beautiful when I saw Phoebe was waiting for me. She leaned against the hood of a brand new Crown Vic. Her left ankle was wrapped and her smile made me warm in all the right places.

"Nice car."

"I figured you could use a ride."

"Thanks. Where are we going?"

Without speaking, she got into the driver's seat, so I eased through the passenger door, grateful for the Crown Vic's soft, comfortable seats. I was again feeling the aches and pains of my wild ride. I was anxious to climb into bed, but I knew there was still some unfinished business.

After a trip up the 405 in which there was remarkably little traffic, Phoebe pulled in front of the Diablo Publishing building. Amazingly, she found a parking space on the street, right next to the front door. We didn't speak as we rode up in the elevator. This building held no good memories for me, and I knew any further confrontation with Edyth would be tough. But I wanted to face her now, so I could get on with my life, and hopefully my writing career.

The elevator doors to Diablo's offices opened to the same view I remembered, and I braced myself for Edyth's screeching voice. We wandered through the main doors and started toward the back where Edyth's office looked out on the city.

But I Wasn't prepared for what I saw when we got there.

Jack and Dick sat in two overstuffed chairs in Edyth's outer office, but they didn't look the way I remembered them. They were both wearing crisply laundered suits with starchy white shirts and silk ties. The last time they posed like this was during the presidential debates.

"Hey Soldier, we were beginning to think you wouldn't make it."

"What are you guys doing here?"

"This is goodbye for us. We wanted to stop by and tell you it's been fun."

I could think of many descriptors of the past few days, and fun wasn't one of them, but I did get two things that would stay with me the rest of my life. I now had eternal love and eternal life, so maybe *fun* wasn't such a bad way to describe it.

"Back at you Mr. Presidents. Hey, what should I do about Edyth?"

Both men stood up and started buttoning their coats. Jack picked a piece of lint off of Dick's lapel, but Nixon swatted his hand away. Then Jack turned to me.

"Take a look around the corner."

I walked toward Edyth's open office door and saw it; the same purplish, goo-ish blast pattern was all over her office. The spandex that had clung so desperately to her body continued to float downward, filling her office with a persistent shower of goo and spandex shrapnel.

A large puddle of the goo had congealed on her desktop, mixing with a large pile of ashes inside her enormous ashtray. But it wasn't just cigarette ashes, I could see that papers had been burned inside the ashtray and I knew what they were. I turned to the fellas.

"Is that my contract?"

"If it isn't, I have lost my touch."

"Well, thanks fellas."

Then they both looked at each other and walked toward me decisively. Jack put his arm on my shoulder.

"One thing Soldier; we are holding you responsible for the girl."

I didn't know what to say. I had never been the *good boyfriend*.

"What do you mean?"

"I mean that we like you and everything, but we came into this situation because we were worried about the girl. She reminds us of our daughters."

"Okay."

"She needs someone *very* special to share her life, and we're not sure you have what it takes."

Dick looked like he was waiting for me to argue with him, but the truth was that I shared his concerns; I didn't know if I had what it took.

"However," Jack continued, "The Lord can give you the strength you need, so depend on Him and you will be just fine."

I was ten percent more relaxed.

"What happens now?"

"We just have to turn in our report to the big man upstairs."

"You mean God?"

"No, I mean Mr. Finkelstein in 4B—Of course I mean God."

They smiled at each other and started toward the door.

"You don't want to be late when you're meeting with the great, *I AM*."

"Will we see you again?"

"Not for awhile, but when we do, it's gonna be a wild party."

Dick turned in my general direction and held out a manuscript. I recognized it as my book that Edyth burned in the trash when I first met her.

"I'd say you need a new ending, and then watch out Harlan Coben!"

I smiled, because Dick had just told me he loved me.

And then they were gone.

When we made it back out to the street, I held Phoebe's hand as we walked to the car. I walked her to the passenger door, but she shook her head.

"Oh no, I'm still driving."

"Okay, but I pick the spots."

"Why do you get to pick the spots? I was going to…"

I held out my arms like Moses, Patch and Charlton Heston had done before me, and when she saw this, it threw her off her game.

"I was going to…"

I kept my arms in Red Sea mode and gave her my best, *shut-up-and-let-me-love-you* expression. She stopped trying to control the lovemaking and looked at me like she had never before noticed how handsome I really was. Then she gave out with the beautiful smile and leaned her elbows on the car to face me.

"So where do you want to go?"

"Right back to that church you took me to. Is that big guy a pastor who can marry people?"

She stopped breathing for a moment, and held her hand to her mouth.

"Yes," she said cautiously.

"Then he's going to marry us, as soon as it's humanly possible."

She smiled, then started crying, then lunged at me in a full-on hugging formation, but I held out my hand for her to stop. I stood there for a moment, holding her at bay. She seemed startled when I did, until I got down on one knee in front of her.

"If, that is, you will agree to be my wife."

She sucked in a big breath, dropped down on her knees with me and kissed me with those lips that redefine words like, *yummy*. I found myself talking while kissing, and that's a first for me.

"Thank you Lord for this woman."

Her smile somehow got a lot bigger. She held on tight and I could feel my temperature rising. Her body next to mine seemed very, very right. I stood, lifted her up and carried her to the Crown Vic. She held my face in her hands tenderly. I could feel her sweet breath on my face, and she leaned in to whisper in my ear.

"We will get a little house, you will write your books, and God will bless us forever."

"Sounds like Heaven."

In case you are wondering…

If you do not know whether or not you own the salvation that Joe received, I urge you to pray the same prayer that he did, inviting the Lord Jesus to become your personal savior. Don't wait another moment because although this story is fictional, the forces of the enemy are very real. The blood of Jesus is the only thing that can wash our sins white as snow, and all we have to do is ask.

I also recommend that you find a good church so that you can get closer to God and increase your blessings. There really is a Rock Church and I really go there. I have grown closer to God at my church and it has changed my life in many beautiful ways. I know you can experience the same happiness. The world cannot provide the blessings you will find at the right church.

I pray that you find Jesus today, so that you can experience the same blessings, the same joy and the same understanding that I have.

In Him,
Ray Sharp, September, 2012